Tempting Adam

Look for these titles by
Shelli Stevens

Now Available:

Trust and Dare

The Seattle Series
Dangerous Grounds (Book 1)
Tempting Adam (Book 2)

Coming Soon:

Taking Chances Series
Anybody but Justin (Book 1)
Luck be Delanie (Book 2)
Protecting Phoebe (Book 3)

Tempting Adam

Shelli Stevens

A SAMHAIN PUBLISHING, LTD. publication.

Samhain Publishing, Ltd.
577 Mulberry Street, Suite 1520
Macon, GA 31201
www.samhainpublishing.com

Tempting Adam
Copyright © 2009 by Shelli Stevens
Print ISBN: 978-1-60504-116-2
Digital ISBN: 1-59998- 912-3

Editing by Laurie Rauch
Cover by Dawn Seewer

This book is a work of fiction. The names, characters, places, and incidents are products of the writer's imagination or have been used fictitiously and are not to be construed as real. Any resemblance to persons, living or dead, actual events, locale or organizations is entirely coincidental.

All Rights Are Reserved. No part of this book may be used or reproduced in any manner whatsoever without written permission, except in the case of brief quotations embodied in critical articles and reviews.

First Samhain Publishing, Ltd. electronic publication: April 2008
First Samhain Publishing, Ltd. print publication: February 2009

Dedication

Thank you to Lacy Danes and Karen Erickson for your thoughts and advice on this novel! You're both fabulous! Thanks to my usual friends and family for your support—to my brother Mark, that summer of visiting you in the hospital is how this book got written. Glad you pulled through! To Jo for your tips on country music/life and even for converting me to become a somewhat listener, to Amanda from Divas for some dancing tips! And to my editor, Laurie, who always has the best advice for making my book that much better!

Chapter One

"Do you want it wet?"

What? Christy Wallace snapped her attention away from the intriguing man standing in front of her, and back to the woman speaking. "I'm sorry?"

"Your cappuccino, Christy. You usually order it wet, but I just wanted to make sure." Madison, who owned the shop, gave her a patient smile even though there was a line of customers to the door.

"Oh. Yes. Wet, please. Thanks, Madison." She flushed, her face giving away the direction of her thoughts. Great, now the entire store probably thought she was some tawdry sex fiend.

Normally the question wouldn't have been such a doozy. She was a regular at Ooo La Latté—had been coming here since shortly after Madison had opened shop—and ordered the same wet cappuccino every day.

But her brain had gone to pot the moment she'd walked through the door and laid eyes on him. The man standing at the end of the line looked like he could've been the stunt double in any James Bond film. Well, a blond Bond. Wait, wasn't Bond blond now anyway? In any case. He had a lean muscular body, hard jaw-line, sensual mouth...and a butt you could bounce a quarter off.

This was the first time she didn't mind waiting ten minutes in line for coffee. Not with the view standing in front of her. Her imagination had gone into overdrive. Those hands...those hands on her body. His body on her body—in her body. The fantasy had gone on and on—only to be broken when Madison confirmed her usual order.

Christy shifted as she waited for her drink, trying to forget about the man who now stood beside her. But, God, he smelled good. She leaned forward slightly and inhaled again. Even over the intense coffee aroma she could smell his cologne. Something woodsy and oh-so-male.

"What's the difference?"

She blinked and then blinked again. Oh God. He was actually talking to her? Her nerves jumped to life.

"Difference in what?"

"Between wet and dry cappuccinos?" he asked, raising an eyebrow at her as he accepted his drink from the barista.

She ran her tongue over suddenly dry lips. His gaze dropped to observe the small movement and her nipples tightened under her sweater.

Christy bit back a groan. What the hell was happening here? She'd been attracted to men before, but never this quick. Sex. Ah, there it was. She needed to get laid. Two years without sex turned her into a sex-starved nympho.

"Wet is with more milk and less foam." She lifted her gaze from his solid chest and up to his amused hazel eyes. Jeez, he was tall. At only five-one, she'd wager he had at least a good foot on her.

"Hmm. I guess I can understand that."

"One wet cappuccino." The barista grinned and handed Christy her drink.

"Thank you." She took it with a grateful smile.

The man next to her looked at her beverage and then gave his a pensive look. "I'm not used to fancy drinks. I just wanted a cup of coffee."

Fancy drinks? Definitely not a local. Christy offered him a smile. "Espresso drinks really aren't all that intimidating. And you know, rumor has it they're even made with coffee."

"I don't think I'd have a clue where to begin."

"Ah." She walked towards one of the leather couches in the shop, elated when he followed. "See, I think what you need is an espresso tutor."

He sat down next to her, stretching his long legs out in front of him. The plush couch seemed suddenly inadequate.

"An espresso tutor, huh?" His mouth curved into an answering smile. "You have any idea where a fellow might be able to get one of those?"

Fellow? Hmm. Christy stared at him. The James Bond fantasy had to go. He was starting to give off more of a Matthew McConaughey vibe. Minus the accent. And Matthew was a genuine hottie in her book.

"I might know one or two," she replied. She was flirting. She was actually flirting! Nate would be so proud.

His smile widened. He took a sip of coffee, and then asked, "What's your name?"

"Christy. Yours?"

"I'm Adam." He glanced down at his coffee and then back up at her. "Christy, how would you like to have dinner with me tonight? You can give me some lessons in espresso."

He was actually asking her out? People didn't date anymore, they hooked up. At least in her experience. And here was this hot-as-heck guy asking her out to dinner a minute after they'd just met. Crap. If she didn't have a previous commitment, she would have been all over dinner with Adam.

"Unfortunately, I'm going to have to say no," she replied, not bothering to hide the regret on her face. She hated the games that went into dating, and had always tried to be honest and straightforward. "I have a different type of lesson to give tonight."

"A different type of lesson?" He took another sip of his coffee. "Sounds interesting. Just what do you teach, Christy?"

"Salsa dancing, actually. But only when I'm not teaching Spanish to high school students."

"A Salsa-dancing, high school teacher?" He looked impressed and amused at the same time. "Well, let me tell you something. We never had any teachers who looked as good as you when I was in high school. I'll bet you get hit on a lot by the students."

Christy laughed, tucking a strand of blonde hair behind her ear self-consciously. *Please let him ask me out for a different day.* "Actually, I did get asked to prom by a senior once."

"I believe it." Adam gave a soft laugh. "Is school out for the kids yet?"

"Friday was our last day." She crossed her legs, and the calf-length dress she wore shifted higher to expose her knees. His gaze followed the movement. Suddenly she was all too aware of his muscular thigh brushing up against hers.

"And now you've got the summer off?" he asked. Was it her? Or did his voice seem a little huskier?

"Yup, and I'm going to savor every moment of it."

He wasn't going to ask her out again. The conversation lulled and Christy lowered her gaze. She should just head out. Besides, she'd requested that maintenance come by to look at the pipes in her apartment. She kind of wanted to be there for that. But the thought of leaving the shop and not seeing Adam again really bugged her.

She stood up, cappuccino in hand. "I should go. It was nice meeting you, Adam."

He rose as well and walked with her towards the door. "Say, where are you teaching these Salsa dancing lessons?"

Christy's pulse jumped with hope as she glanced at him. "Why? Are you thinking of signing up?"

"I'd have to check my schedule."

Right. The disappointment set in. When a guy mentioned a busy schedule, he was looking for a way to brush you off. Reaching into her purse, she pulled out a business card.

"Here's the info," she said, handing it to him. "Come if you want, we could always use more men."

"Thank you, ma'am." Adam revealed his perfect smile again as he took the card and pocketed it.

Christy swallowed hard. Maybe he thought the number on it was a personal line, but it wasn't. Everything on that card was all business or related to it. If this man wanted to pursue her, he would literally have to show up for her class. Yeah right. Like that'd happen.

She found her keys and walked over to her hippie-era Volkswagen Beetle.

"Have yourself a good day, Christy," he called after her. "And thanks for explaining that cappuccino thing to me. Maybe we can go over some more tips sometime."

"Maybe." She waved and climbed into her car. Well, at least he was watching her drive away. And that was probably the last time she'd see him.

"That was fun for the whole five minutes it lasted," she

muttered, stifling her regret as she pulled out of the parking lot and onto the highway.

The sound of Madonna singing "Like a Virgin" rang from her purse, and Christy reached for her cell phone.

"Good morning, Nate," she answered after seeing his picture pop up on her caller ID. "It's only nine-thirty on a Monday morning. Are you sure you should be awake?"

"God, don't remind me." He sighed. "I traded shifts with a coworker, so I had last night off. It was really odd to sleep during the hours that normal humans do."

"I'll bet," Christy replied as she switched lanes. "So I just met this totally hot guy."

"Really? For you or for me?"

"Come on now, when do I ever sound this excited at finding someone for you? He's for me, sweetie."

"Well, I had to check," he grumbled. "All right, spill it. Give me the details."

"I met him at Ooo La Latté a few minutes ago. I guess—now that I think about it—there's not a lot to tell." She switched her phone from one ear to another. "I saw him in line and started having these totally kinky thoughts about him. I think he figured it out, because the next thing I knew we were sitting on the couch flirting over coffee. Sorry. I had cappuccino, he had coffee."

"Nice. Did you get his number?"

"Err, no," she hesitated. "He asked me out to dinner tonight, but I told him I was busy."

"What? Christy! You didn't accept the date? What were you thinking?"

"Uh, hello, I was thinking about my Salsa classes tonight. Remember? I gave him my card, though, and told him he could take my class if he wanted to see me. Pretty doubtful that he'll actually show." Christy sighed. "But, I can't brush off my commitments for a guy who'll probably turn out to just be another dud."

"You're smart like that, Christy. Hey, how did that one guy turn out? That guy Lannie was trying to set you up with? The best man from her wedding?"

"Oh, right. Gabe." Christy frowned. He'd actually been a pretty decent guy whom she wouldn't have minded getting to know better. That is if he hadn't already been head over heels for Maddie—the owner of the coffee shop.

"So was he cute?"

"He was cute." She sighed. "Cute and taken. They always are."

"Well, that's a bummer." Nate was quiet for a moment. "Hey, there is a reason I called. Can you meet me for breakfast tomorrow? We need to do some real talking."

"Real talking, huh? As opposed to just chatting about men? Sounds serious."

"Um, it kind of is."

"Oh. Really? Do you want me to come over now?" Christy slowed her car, ready to flip a U-turn and head to his apartment on Broadway.

"No, not now. I'm meeting someone for lunch in a couple of hours."

"A date?"

"Sort of. I met him in a gay chat room."

"Nice. Good luck with him. I want to hear all about that too at breakfast tomorrow."

"You will. Where did you want to meet?"

His voice, which had been animated after mentioning his

date, again became more somber. Hmm. Just what, exactly, was this real talk going to entail?

"Why don't we meet at Bob's Café," she suggested. "I've been craving a six-egg omelet."

"Damn, where do you put it all? I hate that place. I smell like grease when we leave."

"So shower when you get home. Grease becomes me."

"Fine. I'll meet you there around ten."

"Nine."

"I have to work tonight!" he protested. "Let me get a few hours of sleep in before we meet."

"I have errands up the yin-yang tomorrow. Nine."

Nate sighed. "Nine-thirty?"

"Done. I'll see you tomorrow. Good luck with your date," she said and flipped her phone shut.

Well, at least one of them was having some success with men. It was probably better if Adam didn't show tonight. She'd have to be nuts to put her heart out on the line again. She'd only just gotten over her last relationship. Really. It was best just to forget the whole coffee episode.

Adam who?

"Exactly," she muttered. Now. What could she wear tonight that was cute?

ଌ

"Hello, gorgeous. Love the outfit." Carlos, the owner of the studio, stretched out his hands to greet her.

"This old thing? I got it at a shop on Broadway." Christy took his hands and leaned forward to give him a kiss on each cheek. She didn't have to stretch too far, because Carlos was only a few inches taller than her.

His nose wrinkled. "Oh yes. I forgot about your habit of buying used clothes."

"Second-hand shopping. And don't knock it 'til you've tried it." She grinned. "Besides, I'm a teacher living in downtown Seattle. Where do you think most of my money's going?"

"You should move out of that dump," he grumbled as he went to fiddle with the CD player. "Get a nice apartment in the suburbs for half the price and save some money."

"Probably. But Pioneer Square is right in the middle of the tourist and party scene. My apartment might be a dump, but it's highly desired."

"Party scene? I thought you gave up flirting with the Navy boys who come over from Bremerton?" He gave her a sideways glance.

"I'll have you know that I've been in remission from Navy men for two years and counting now."

"Good girl. Just keep your feet grounded, *niña*. Shall we warm up a bit before the students start arriving?" he asked, hitting the play button on the CD player beside him.

"Sounds good." A rush of adrenaline kicked in. The rhythm of the music got into her blood and put her in another realm.

As the sultry, upbeat Latin music started to fill the room, Christy unzipped her sweatshirt and threw it on a chair. Her tank top and skirt combo was sexy, yet practical. The sexy part was needed in case Adam showed up. The practical bit was for the dancing itself.

She stepped towards his outstretched hands. They waited for the music to come around, and on the second beat they were off.

The dance was second nature. Her feet and body knew exactly what to do and how to do it. She followed Carlos's lead, spinning and breaking when he guided her to.

They'd been dancing fifteen minutes when people began to arrive for the seven o'clock class. Christy took little notice, following Carlos as he continued the dance.

Then her gaze drifted beyond Carlos's shoulders and landed on a man standing near the door. *Oh God.* She bit her lip, but was unable to stop the immediate smile. Amazing, he'd actually showed. Her pulse, already fast from dancing, went into overdrive. Heat spread throughout her body.

"That's some smile you've got there," Carlos said. "Any reason why?"

"He came."

"He?" Carlos spun her, so that he now had the view of the door to the studio. "I assume you mean the only guy here who isn't a senior citizen, gay, or with another woman?"

"Yeah." She kept her voice low. "The tall, lean, blond one."

"Not too lean." Carlos gave Adam a thoughtful glance. "He looks like he's got some muscle on him."

And didn't she notice! Christy giggled. "Don't let your wife hear you talking like that. She might get the wrong idea."

"Serena is very happy." Carlos's expression turned smug. "She has no room for complaints."

Christy rolled her eyes. "You men, you're all the same."

The song came to an end and so did their dance. The room filled with a smattering of applause from their students.

Christy stepped back from Carlos and lifted her gaze towards Adam. He was leaning against the wall, looking relaxed and curious. When she met his eyes, though, his expression was more guarded. Hmm. What was he thinking about?

She raised an eyebrow at him in acknowledgment, and then turned to look over the rest of her new students. There were a few twenty-somethings, a few seniors, and a handful of middle-aged couples. No doubt the wives had dragged their husbands out after watching one of the dancing movies or television shows that were so popular now.

"Welcome everyone," Carlos called out, walking over to the group. "I am Carlos, and this is Christina. We will be teaching you to dance Salsa for the next week. This is the high-intensity class where you learn it all in six days. Are you ready?"

There were a bunch of affirmative replies from the small crowd. Christy turned her glance back towards Adam. She held back a laugh. He was suddenly looking towards the exit. *Ah, so he was having second thoughts. Well, she'd just have to make this as easy on him as possible.*

"All right." Carlos turned to face Christy. "You go ahead and take it from here, *niña.*"

"Thanks." She gave him a big smile, taking a nervous breath before turning back towards the group. "Hello, everyone. Why don't you grab a partner. It doesn't have to be boy-girl if we don't have an equal ratio."

Christy strode towards Adam and took his hand. *Yikes, was that a shock?* The tingle where their hands connected moved up her arm as she led him onto the floor. His hands were large and callused. He probably did hard work and didn't mind getting dirty. God that was sexy.

She immediately envisioned those rough hands cupping her breasts, while his long fingers teased her nipples. Swallowing hard, she tried to bring her focus back to the dance lessons she was about to teach.

"Are you sure you're supposed to be doing this?" Adam asked, looking pleased that she'd chosen him. "Shouldn't you be dancing with your other guy?"

"He's not my guy," she replied. "And, no, we're supposed to split our talents up and grab the newbies."

"Well, aren't I the lucky one." His widening smile and deep voice had her mind going all muddy. She literally had to shake her head to clear it.

"I'm surprised you even showed. I didn't take you for the type of guy who wanted to learn how to dance Salsa."

"Now, Christy, that's why we need to get to know each other a little better."

The fluttering in her belly started. "I can't wait."

Remember why you're here, Christy. As much as you may want to, it's not to flirt with Adam. At least not during class. She cut the eye contact to check out how the students were pairing up.

Nice, they had an equal amount of females and males. Carlos was standing next to a blushing woman who couldn't have been a day under seventy.

"Okay, now that everyone has a partner, let me tell you a little bit about Salsa dancing," Christy began. "There are four beats to a bar, and thus four dance steps to a bar of music. Okay?"

Most of the people nodded that they understood.

"When you're dancing Salsa, you're going to feel the urge to start on the first beat. Don't. In Salsa, your feet only move on beats two and four."

Christy nodded at Carlos to hit the music again. When the music began, she turned to face Adam with an amused smile.

"All right, partner," she murmured. "Let's see how quick you learn."

He tilted his head. "Just try me, darlin'."

Weak knees don't make for good dancing, Christy told herself, and pushed aside the unwanted feminine reaction.

"There are two basic movements to Salsa dancing," Christy went on, trying not to obsess about the sexy man she was teaching how to dance. "The forward basic movement, and the backward basic movement."

The couples who were watching her and Adam began to mimic their moves.

"Generally, the man will lead. The lady facing the man will perform steps complementing his. If he moves his left foot forward, she moves her right foot back."

Adam looked up from his feet, which he'd been focusing on, and back at her.

"Yes," she told him before he could ask. "I'm the man right now."

"A little role reversal." He clucked his tongue. "See, I could tell right away you were a kinky girl."

Christy stumbled. *Don't think about sex. Not now. Bad timing, very bad timing.*

She went on, struggling to keep her voice steady. "The men will step forward and tap left, then rock back on the right foot, and finish by stepping backing on the left. Women, go ahead and mirror these steps, but when he's going forward, you're going back."

Adam shook his head. "All right, you win. I've been confused since you started talking about numbers."

Christy threw back her head and laughed, continuing to guide him through the movements. "You're doing all right, just smile and try to get through it."

Chapter Two

Adam wondered how he managed to do just that. Smile and dance Salsa like he really gave a damn. He didn't care an ounce for Salsa dancing. Now the woman he was dancing with, he cared a great deal about getting to know her better.

Earlier he'd switched partners, and found himself shuffling around with various other women. But his thoughts had stayed with Christy, and it wasn't long before she returned to his arms.

She was what his dad would refer to as *enchanting*. With her laugh, her subtle flirting, and how absolutely gorgeous she was. Those wide blue eyes and pale blonde hair. And the smattering of freckles on her nose made him want to kiss the upturned tip.

She was a little more petite than most of the women he'd dated. She was almost tiny, by his standards. But she was rounded in all the right places and had breasts that would be a perfect fit for his hands. And, Lord, that gently rounded ass she'd displayed to him when she did her flirty turns in the dance.

"Almost done," she whispered as they came inches away from each other. "Can you last for a few more minutes?"

Every time they came in close contact, he could smell her perfume. She smelled sweet, almost edible.

"Darlin', I can go all night."

Christy winced, her expression turning wry. "I suppose I set myself up for that one."

"I suppose you did," he agreed with a smile. "You going to let me take you out for dinner after this?"

"Dinner?" She raised an eyebrow. "It's nearly eight o'clock. I ate before I came."

Adam wasn't deterred. He didn't want this night to end when class did. "How about a snack before bed?"

Her eyelashes fell, hiding her expression. "I...I have to get up early in the morning. I'd better not."

The disappointment stung. What was going on with her? Had she just been stringing him along? Was she playing hard to get? That didn't seem right. She'd seemed interested in him—he'd seen her response in the coffee shop this morning. The way her nipples had gone hard under her sweater. The blood flowed to his crotch at the memory of it, and he abruptly turned his thoughts back to what might have spooked her.

Maybe she just wasn't experienced with men. But she'd certainly flirted like she was. Maybe he'd just been too forward. That seemed a little more likely.

The song ended. Christy released his hands to step away from him.

"Congratulations." She raised her voice to address the class. "You've just completed your first Salsa lesson. I'll see you all tomorrow night."

Adam stood there. Should he cut his losses and leave? Or try to talk to her more? Christy had already crossed the room and picked up a hand towel from the bench, using it to wipe over her face, which was amusing, since she hadn't even broken a sweat.

He stopped hesitating and walked over to her. She looked

up, seeming surprised that he was still here.

"Did you have fun?" Her question and tone were equally polite.

"It was interesting," he compromised. "I'm sure I'll pick up more tomorrow night."

"You're coming back?" she asked, and then her cheeks tinged pink. "I mean, I think you should. They're week-long classes. I just wasn't sure you'd want to."

"When I start something, I finish it," he promised, enjoying watching the flush in her cheeks deepen.

Christy tucked a strand of hair behind her ear. He'd noticed she did that when she was nervous or embarrassed.

"All right, well I'd better head out." She slipped a bag over her shoulder and waved goodbye to Carlos who was locking up.

Adam kept pace with her as she walked out the door. "Let me see you to your car."

"Thanks, that's sweet of you." She cast him a sideways look. "Do you have a long drive home?"

"I'm not from Seattle. I'm just in town for the week."

Disappointment flashed across her face before she could turn away to hide it. Hmm, so she wasn't looking for a one-night stand. Then again, neither was he. Not with her. She intrigued him like no woman had before. One night with Christy would be like watching half of the Super Bowl.

"But I have a lot of business here. I come back often."

Her smile seemed a bit forced now. "Well, you picked a good week to visit. Now you get to be one of my students."

"It's been a long time since I was a student," he admitted and stopped when she reached her car. "But I'm mighty glad you're my instructor, Christy."

"Why is that?"

The sudden huskiness in her voice was a good indication that she wasn't immune to him. Despite his decision not to rush her, he was going to touch her. At least once.

"Because you're every man's fantasy teacher," he said with a laugh. "And I'm going to kiss you now. If you don't mind."

Her lips parted in surprise, and before she could answer, he lowered his mouth to hers.

Her soft lips sent a stab of desire through him, which only increased when he slipped his tongue through the seam of her lips.

She tried to wrap her arms around his neck, but wasn't tall enough. He laughed when her fingernails instead clutched at the top of his shoulders. She was so small, yet so lush. He settled his hands on her hips to pull her closer. Her nipples were hard, he could feel them brushing against his chest.

Adam stroked his tongue against hers a few more times, and then retreated. Slowing the kiss to just small brushes of his mouth over hers. He didn't want to spook her anymore than he already had earlier. When he finally lifted his head, her eyes were closed.

"I'll see you tomorrow night, okay?" He drew the pad of his thumb over her swollen lips.

"Okay," she murmured, and opened her eyes to look up at him.

Her blue gaze was hazy with arousal, and his confidence surged. There was no doubt about it. She might have gone all shy for a moment, but she still wanted him.

༄

"Good morning, sunshine," Christy called out as she

strolled into Bob's Café the next morning. The smell of grease was thick in the air, and almost every table was full. Nate stood in the entryway, waiting for her to join him.

"Is it?" He yawned.

"Well, it is for those of us who didn't have to work all night."

"Hey, I wanted this little meeting to be later in the day."

She kissed his cheek. "I know, I know. Thanks for accommodating me. Let's sit down."

Christy led him slowly through the crowded restaurant.

"Why are you so damn cheerful, anyway?" Nate grumbled, his dark eyes narrowing with suspicion.

"He showed up last night."

Nate frowned and tilted his head, then his eyes widened. "Oh! The guy you met at the coffee shop? No kidding!"

"You kids need to see a menu?" Doris, their usual waitress, stopped in front of their booth and gave them a brief smile. Her lips were coated in an obnoxiously pink lipstick shade that hadn't been popular since the eighties.

"No, we're good." Christy grinned and flipped over her coffee mug. "Regular coffee for me."

"You want coffee, honey?" Doris asked Nate, and then turned her face away to emit a haggard-sounding cough. "Damn cigarettes."

Nate cringed. "I'm fine, thanks."

Doris tilted the pot of coffee over Christy's upturned mug. Christy's expression remained neutral, even though every fiber in her being protested the drinking of bad coffee. She had yet to find a breakfast joint that served decent coffee. But bad or good, she needed her caffeine.

"All right, you two need a minute?" Doris asked after filling the stained mug to the brim.

Nate shook his head. "I'll have a mushroom and green pepper omelet, made with egg whites only. Oh, and tomato slices instead of hash browns."

Doris's lips twitched and her eyebrows rose, but she said nothing and look expectantly at Christy.

"I'll do a six-egg, bacon, cheddar, and sour cream omelet," Christy replied immediately. "And could I get extra hash browns with that?"

"Would you like that heart disease for here or to go?" Nate asked after Doris had walked off. "Jeez, you and my family. You all eat like crap."

"Just because you're eager to convert to being a health nut, doesn't mean the rest of us have to."

"Well, sweetie..." he rolled his eyes, "...I don't know how you can eat an omelet made with a half a dozen eggs—loaded with fat and calories—and still stay a size four."

"Genetics and a great metabolism. Don't you just hate me?" Christy smirked and drank another sip of the bad coffee.

"I would if you weren't so damn cute." He sighed. "I hope she remembers the tomatoes instead of hash browns."

"She's never forgotten."

"Yeah." He scowled. "But there's always a first time."

"My, aren't we grouchy today?" Christy crossed her legs and gave him a narrowed look. "What's going on? Does this have something to do with your date yesterday?"

His face changed so quickly she had to laugh.

"Yesterday was amazing. We sat talking over the same cup of coffee for two hours," he confessed, leaning forward eagerly. "We have so much in common. And did I mention how hot he is? He's a Drama major at Cornish."

"Wow, sounds promising."

Nate sighed and stared at his hands. "I just really think that it could be different with him."

"Yeah? I hear you on that one."

His attention snapped back to her. "That's right. Tell me about the boy."

"Grown man, thank you very much." Christy giggled. "He's wickedly good-looking, a charming flirt, and he makes me forget my own name when he kisses me."

"You've kissed?" Nate gasped. "You're one up on me. He sounds fabulous, Christy. Hang on to him for awhile."

"I would, but he's not a Seattleite." Her stomach clenched at the reminder. "He's just visiting. So now the question is—do I have amazing sex for a few days and then see what happens? Or do I just call it quits while I'm still ahead?"

"Uh, no brainer here. Have some sex, Christy. Before your hymen grows back. How long has it been anyway?"

"Not that long," she protested and then averted her gaze. "A couple of years. Maybe."

"God, I can't even go a couple of days without masturbating."

"I never said that I don't masturbate. And of course you think about sex more often, gay or not, you're still a guy."

"Anyway!" He rolled his eyes. "What are you going to do?"

"I have no idea," she admitted with a despondent look. "I get the feeling that if I try to have casual sex with him, I'm going to end up getting really hurt. I think I like him too much for it to be casual."

"Hmm, I see your dilemma. Well, my advice to you is to play it by ear," Nate told her. "If he shows up to class tonight—"

"He told me he would."

"Then go out with him afterwards and see how it goes. How you feel." He paused, looking thoughtful. "Ask yourself 'Can I live the rest of my life knowing that I gave up a few nights passion with this man?' and if you think you could look back with no regrets on passing, you've got your answer. But if you think you'd always wonder... I say go for it."

"Thanks, Nate. That's very philosophical."

Doris returned with plates full of heaping food.

Christy grabbed her fork and then dove into her omelet with great enthusiasm. Mmm. Bacon. A few minutes later she glanced up to see Nate watching her with disdain.

"Shut up." She waved her fork at him. "I don't want to hear it." She took another bite and closed her eyes, moaning her approval. "Now," she said a moment later. "When you called me yesterday, you told me we had to have a real talk. Are we still going to?"

"Yes, we are. I was just putting it off," Nate replied, liberally sprinkling pepper over his washed-out excuse for an omelet.

"Okay. So, what's the deal?"

"I need a favor," he said slowly, pushing a slice of tomato around his plate. His knuckles were white from how tight he held the fork.

"Hmm. It's not one of those things where I have to get dressed up in a cow costume again, is it?" A vision of that children's fair he'd suckered her into years ago flickered through her head.

"No, I kinda wish it was." He paused. "It's a little more complex."

He was really uncomfortable, Christy realized. This wasn't a favor he wanted to ask for.

She touched his hand. "You know I'll help you out in any

way that I can. What do you need?"

He took a deep breath. "Well, my family's coming out to Seattle to visit. They should be arriving any time now."

"Your parents?" she asked in surprise. "They're coming over from Eastern Washington?"

"Yeah, and my older brother." His mouth tightened.

"But that's great," she said and shook her head. "I've still never met your family. And you've seen my mom a dozen times at least. Do I get an introduction this time around?"

"Yes. But, Christy... I haven't told them."

"Told them?" She took another bite of her breakfast. Then she looked up suddenly. Wait a minute. Did he mean...?

"That's right. They don't know," he mumbled, his expression tight.

"So, they still think you're a skirt-chasing, lusty country boy?" Christy asked, letting the air whoosh out between pursed lips. She shook her head and gave him a sympathetic smile. "And you're going to break it to them when they're here?"

"Well, that's just it." He averted his gaze. "That's where you come in."

"Where I come in?" Her eyebrows rose. "I hope you're not asking me to break the news. I can just see it. 'Hi, I'm Christy, Nate's friend. Great to finally meet you. Oh, by the way, your son prefers men. Now, who wants to visit the Space Needle?'"

"I'm not asking you to tell them anything," he said, his whole body tense. "I'm asking you to be my girlfriend."

Chapter Three

It took a second before Christy could speak. "I'm sorry? Did I miss something? Or were you just pretending to be gay for the past couple of years?"

"Of course not." He gave an impatient sigh. "Please, I'm being serious here, Christy."

"You're being serious." She nodded. "Yet you want to introduce me to your family as your girlfriend?"

"Yes," he replied reluctantly. "It'll only be for a week."

"One week." Her jaw flexed with annoyance. "Tell me something. Do you *ever* plan on telling them?"

"Yes, of course. It's just a bad time right now."

She gave him a disbelieving look.

He sighed and looked away. "My dad had a heart attack last year and just underwent a bypass a few months ago. The news would probably get him so upset he'd give himself another attack."

"Nate—"

He turned back to face her, leaning forward. "My family is ultra conservative. They're Republicans, Christy. Church-going Republicans."

Christy rolled her eyes, knowing he was really desperate if he was pulling out the conservative Republicans bit. She sighed, feeling the weight of his request sitting heavily on her.

"I don't like this, Nate. Why don't you just pretend to be a straight single guy this week?"

"Because they're starting to wonder why I've never had a girlfriend," he muttered. "I'll tell them, I promise. I just don't want to risk my dad's health right now."

He looked so desperate, so stressed out. She closed her eyes with a sigh. "It's just one week?"

"Just one week," he replied quickly.

"Okay, I'll do it. But you'd better tell them within the year, because I am *not* going through this again."

Nate's relief was obvious. The tension in his shoulders eased, and the color in his face returned. "You're the best, Christy. If I weren't gay I'd marry you in heartbeat."

"I wouldn't marry you. You're too healthy." She picked her fork up again. "Now give me some background on your family."

"What do you want to know?"

"What do your parents do? What does your brother do? Does he live with them?"

"Live with them?" Nate laughed. "My brother has his own house. He lives a few miles down the road from my parents' farm."

"Oh my God, your parents live on a farm?" Her eyes widened as images of the country life flitted through her head. "That's so cute."

"Yeah, can't you just see me running around milking cows?"

"Uh, no, I'm actually not getting a visual on that." Christy smiled. "So they run a farm. That's how they make their income?"

"Sort of," he mumbled, finishing off the rest of his

tomatoes. "My brother runs a little fruit business and they work for him doing the accounting and paperwork."

"That's sweet."

Doris came over to refill her coffee and Christy leaned back in her seat until she'd finished. When she disappeared again, she focused back to Nate.

"What's your brother like?"

Nate snorted. "Basically an overgrown jock, country bumpkin who does most of his thinking with his dick."

"Hmm." She didn't bother to hide her sarcasm. "It sounds like you two have a *great* relationship."

"Well, it's a little hard, all right? He's just everything my parents expect me to be."

"Ah." Christy nodded, starting to feel sorry for him despite her intentions not to. "So, when are we meeting them?"

"Tomorrow for lunch?"

"Want to bring them here?" she teased.

"God, no!" he shuddered. "I'll talk to them tonight and give you a call with the details. I'm not sure where they'll want to go. They love doing the tourist stuff when they come out here."

"Just let me know and I'll meet you wherever you need me. *Sweetie.*"

"Oh, Christy, I can't thank you enough."

Christy picked up her coffee. "Don't thank me, you're buying my breakfast."

ଚ

Nate had made a good point at breakfast. Would she regret it if she didn't act on this passion with Adam?

She still hadn't decided. It doesn't mean anything that she'd shaved, put lotion on her entire body, dabbed perfume…

"Oh, hell, who am I kidding?" she muttered and dragged out the cliché little black dress.

Throwing it on the bed, she went to her dresser and pulled open her underwear drawer. Why not go all out? She grabbed a zipped-up plastic bag labeled 'guaranteed to get some'. It was a lingerie set that she'd never worn, but put aside for a special occasion.

Now seemed special enough. Christy unzipped it and pulled out the red lacy thong and matching bra.

She put on the lingerie and dress, and then checked the mirror. Very nice. It emphasized her waist, and made her breasts look bigger. Not bad for a twelve-dollar dress. God, she loved thrift shopping.

She went back to her closet and pulled out a pair of black stiletto heels. The shoes had been full price—some things were just worth saving up for.

Christy glanced at the clock. Yikes. Only time for a quick makeup job.

A few minutes later she locked the door behind her and headed downstairs to her car. She stepped over the usual drunk who was seated against the building leering at her, and hurried to her car.

She arrived at the studio five minutes later. The lights were on and she could see Carlos stretching inside.

"Hey there," she called out as she passed through the doors.

"Dios Mio!" Carlos shouted as he saw her. "Either you've got a hot date afterwards, or you're loco for that man you were dancing with last night."

Christy gave him a slow smile. "Why not both?"

"That poor guy." He shook his head. "He's going to have to spend the next hour dancing with a colossal hard-on."

She gave a delicate shudder. "Careful, don't get me all excited before he gets here."

"You're right, that's his job." Carlos flicked on the music. "Let's warm up."

Adam slammed the door to his pickup and started towards the door to the dance studio. There was already a crowd of people standing near the entrance, staring at the couple on the floor. He lifted his gaze to get a look. He sucked in a quick breath, feeling his stomach clench.

The dress Christy wore was gravity-defying as she went into a spin. It lifted off her thighs and exposed an amazing amount of leg for someone so petite. Her creamy breasts were playing peek-a-boo out of the low-cut bodice. Oh Lord.

Stop looking at her tits. He turned his gaze to her feet. Those heels. Sweet Jesus. He was about an inch away from a full erection.

He stepped back into the doorway, breathing in the city air to clear his senses. Maybe that wasn't the best idea, city air wasn't exactly refreshing. He turned his gaze over to the Seattle skyline, which was coated in pink from the sunset.

God. How was he ever going to get through an hour lesson pressed up against Christy's compact curves? He groaned. Why couldn't she have been a basket-weaving teacher instead? Of course, he probably would have found something arousing about that too.

Adam closed his eyes, counted to fifty, and when his

erection had subsided to a less obvious level, he went inside.

Carlos and Christy were just finishing up, and instructing people to find a partner. Christy's gaze searched the room—he hoped for him—and finally she saw him. Relief crossed her face, and her expression grew downright sultry.

Whatever had spooked her last night was gone. Tonight she looked like a woman who'd made the decision to take a lover. Him. A carnal wave of lust shot through him as he strode across the room towards her.

"I think you are about the sexiest woman I've ever laid eyes on." His gaze raked over her as he reached out to take her hands. "Will you have dinner with me tonight?"

"Funny you should ask," she said breathlessly. "Because I seem to have forgotten to eat before I came."

No excuses this time. She must want this as much as he did. "Ain't that something? It just seems to be my lucky day."

"I'd say so." She ran her tongue over her glossy lips, and he bit back a groan at the erotic movement. "But we can't go for another hour. Can you make it through class?"

Now there was the question of the hour. He pulled her body closer to his. "I sure intend to try."

"That's what I like to hear, cowboy."

"Cowboy? What makes you think I'm a cowboy?" he asked, raising an eyebrow.

"I was just being cute. But now that you mention it, you do kind of give off that cowboy vibe." Christy pulled on his hand, leading him out to the middle of the floor.

"I like to ride horses," he admitted.

"Anything else you like to ride?" she murmured against his ear.

Adam's dick went hard. Again. Thank God they were

pressed close together. At least this way the entire class couldn't see his erection. Christy's soft laughter indicated that she hadn't missed it though. She turned towards the rest of the class.

"Hello again, everybody!" she called out. "Welcome to the second night of your Salsa lessons."

There was a smattering of applause along with murmurs of excitement.

"All right, let's start where we left off last night."

Carlos hit the music, and steered his partner—the blushing senior citizen—out onto the floor.

Christy started calling out the directions to the steps of the dance.

The next hour was hell. Her sweet perfume teased his nostrils. Her breasts brushed the side of his arm every few minutes. Adam welcomed the breaks from her when they had to rotate partners. It gave him a few minutes to have a coherent thought.

Finally it was eight o'clock. Adam's adrenaline kicked in. Christy's gaze locked with his. She looked nervous, but the glint in her eyes showed her excitement as well.

"Can you lock up, Carlos?" she asked without taking her eyes off Adam.

"Sure can. Have fun, kids."

Adam took her hand in his, and led her out the door.

"So, where are we going?" he asked, pausing in front of his truck.

She tucked a strand of hair behind her ear. "I happen to be a pretty good cook. Why don't you follow me back to my place and I'll whip us up some dinner."

His mouth curved into a smile. She was bringing him back

to her place. If he'd had any doubts of her intentions, she'd just put them to rest. "I do love home cooking."

"Good." She pointed to her car. "I'm over there. Just follow me. It's about a five-minute drive and it's street parking, so take whatever you can find."

She hurried over to her car, her cute ass swinging, before she climbed inside with a tiny wave. Adam got behind the wheel of his truck and pulled out after her.

The drive following her seemed to take an obscene amount of time, although it had probably only lasted a few minutes.

Once outside her building, it took a few more minutes before he could find a spot to park in. Christy stood on the dark sidewalk waiting for him. She'd taken her hair down and it fell in waves to her shoulders. *Damn, she was sexy.*

After he finally locked the car door and turned on the alarm, he jogged over to her.

"That's the first time I've ever used the alarm on my truck." He glanced over his shoulder. Hopefully it would be okay here.

"Seriously?" she laughed. "Where do you live, cowboy, Kansas?"

"Not quite." He took her hand and followed her into the brick building, almost tripping over the man who was passed out with a bottle in his hand.

"Sorry about that," she said with an apologetic look. "It kind of comes with the territory."

"No problem," he said neutrally. She had to do this regularly? Avoid drunks outside her building? The thought made him uneasy.

They climbed the stairs to her apartment.

She unlocked the door. "Come on in," she invited, flipping on the light switch. "And make yourself at home while I figure out what to make us for dinner."

Adam walked into the center of the room and looked around. The flowers on the table could account for the floral smell. Was there another room somewhere? There was only a narrow door that was open, revealing a tiny bathroom. Hmm. Nope, this was it.

His gaze ran over the living room again. The futon was probably a couch. Most likely her bed, too. How much did a studio run in downtown Seattle, anyway? Best not ask. He didn't want to come across as rude.

The smallness of the studio also added to the intimacy of it. He was here. With Christy. God, he couldn't wait to touch her.

"What do you like to eat?" she asked from the kitchen.

Adam turned to look back at her, a kinky response on the tip of his tongue. *Don't shock her to her toes just yet.*

"I eat just about anything, darlin'. 'Less it's tofu."

"You're in luck, I hate tofu."

He watched her pull two steaks out of the fridge. Had she planned this ahead of time? Or maybe she just really liked meat.

"You can sit down if you want, turn on the television or something."

She sounded a little nervous again, so Adam sat down on the futon to put her more at ease.

"Tell me something about yourself," she asked as she brushed some kind of sauce over the raw steaks. "Something exciting."

"Something exciting?" Was he exciting? Hmm. He could tell her about his business, but that seemed a little heavy. He'd go with the side job. "I'm a volunteer firefighter. Is that exciting?"

Christy looked up from the steaks and gave him a slow

smile. "Oh, God, yes. I think firefighters are an incredible turn on. What girl doesn't?"

He smiled, letting his gaze drift over Christy in her tiny dress and four-inch heels, getting ready to broil them a steak dinner. Now that was a turn on.

Christy put the steaks in the oven and then started the rice cooking. When she came back into the living room, she sat down beside him on the futon. Almost close enough so that their thighs touched.

"Hi," she murmured giving him another glance from under her eyelashes.

"Hey there," he answered, tracing the back of his fingers across her cheek. So soft. She seemed to be getting more comfortable, but why not speed things along a little?

She leaned her cheek against his hand. Her tongue snuck out to sweep over her bottom lip before retreating back inside.

Adam dropped his gaze to her lower lip and brought his finger up to trace it.

"You've got a very sensual mouth, darlin'."

"You think so?" Her lips parted and she sucked one of his fingers into the moist interior.

Adam sucked in a breath. There went the last of her shyness.

"You keep doing that—" his voice dropped an octave, becoming harsher, "—and we won't make it 'til dinner."

Christy's tongue ran over his finger one last time, before she released it and gave him a thoughtful glance.

"I've read some romance books, and they always say something bizarre like 'his voice was smooth like whiskey' and I never understood it." She shook her head. "But I think I just got it. If tequila could talk, you'd be its voice."

Adam threw back his head and laughed with real amusement. "That was random. Is that all you learned reading romance novels?"

"Of course not," she admonished him with a wicked grin. "I've learned many other interesting things. And if you're a good boy, I may just try them out on you."

Adam's laughter dried up. How long would it take for him to turn this futon into a bed? Damn. He just wanted to lay her down and do things to her that would make her head spin. And then let her do the same to him.

He'd never met a woman like Christy. Flirty, beautiful, and a mind that seemed in tune with a man's way of thinking.

She was a rarity that most men would love to get their hands on. Why was she single—not that he was complaining—and why had she chosen him?

"I think I'll check on the steaks."

She practically jumped off the couch to get back to the kitchen. There it was again. That rapid change from seductress to shy school teacher.

Hmm. That's right. There was still that school teacher fantasy. Or was that the schoolgirl fantasy? Either way, they both were a turn on.

"They're done."

Adam turned to see her leaning over the oven with an oven mitt. Her dress had risen up to expose the backs of her thighs. He closed his eyes to shut out the image. *Down, boy. You still have to get through dinner.*

"Do you want wine?" she offered as she set two plates down at the table in the corner.

"That'd be fine, thank you. Can I help you with anything?"

"No, I'm good. Why don't you grab a seat at the table and

I'll bring it out to you in a second."

Christy waited until Adam sat down at the table, her heart pounding a mile a minute. He looked out of place in her girly apartment. He was just...such a guy. Tall, broad-shouldered, and sexy as sin in his jeans and T-shirt.

She slid one of the sizzling steaks onto his plate, her arm brushing his broad shoulder in the process. She ignored the tingling sensation.

Hopefully he liked her cooking. Wait, why was she even worrying about that? She shook her head. They were about to eat a nice steak dinner. After dinner they'd put their plates in the sink. After that they'd...she swallowed hard and fought the rush of nerves. They'd have sex. That's what. And it was about freaking time.

Nate was right. Didn't some religions consider you a born-again virgin if you went a year without sex?

She grabbed utensils for them both, and then walked back to the table to sit down.

"You're not going to make me eat my vegetables?" he teased, glancing down at his plate.

Christy's lips twitched. "I'm more of a fruit girl, but next time I'll pick up some broccoli just for you."

"I'd rather you didn't. This looks great, Christy. Thank you."

Christy felt her stomach warm at the compliment. He dug into his food with obvious pleasure, groaning in approval. She wondered if he made love with the same kind of freedom. The thought sent a stab of desire through her that wound up straight between her legs. Yes, deciding to go to bed with Adam was a good choice. She crossed her legs and turned to her dinner.

"I didn't expect this caliber of a meal when you invited me back." His teeth sunk into a piece of steak. "A woman who's not only beautiful, but can cook. Tell me something, how come you're not married?"

Shitty-ass luck, she wanted to reply, but shrugged instead. "I'm not sure I'm the marrying kind."

Adam reared back. "Now that sounds like something a man would say."

Christy rolled her eyes and picked up her wine glass. "Come on, right now you're on my good side. Don't get all stereotypical on me and make me have to kick your ass."

He stared at her for a moment. Yikes, had she gone too far? Carlos and Nate were used to her blunt humor—often enjoyed it—but Adam barely knew her.

And yet you're going to bed with him? a reasonable voice inside her asked in disbelief. *Damn straight, but I'll be safe about it.* She snapped out of her internal conversation to the realization that he was laughing.

"I'd love to see you try, darlin'. I really would."

Try what? She frowned, trying to remember. Oh, that's right. The whole kicking his ass bit. It could be fun. Not that she actually had a chance in hell at winning though.

Christy gave him a sideways glance. "Careful, I just might take you up on that. And then we'll see who ends up on top."

"Hmm, in that case I may lose on purpose."

She laughed, ignoring the image that popped into her head, and glanced at his nearly empty plate. "I can't believe you've almost eaten everything. I must be a slow eater."

"Nope, I'm just fast." He stood up and took his plate to the sink, then started to wash it.

"You don't have to do that," she protested. "I'll get it once I've finished."

"No can do," he replied, rinsing the plate fully before sticking it into the dishwasher. "You cooked, so I'll do the dishes."

Was she dreaming? She watched in amazement as he proceeded to clean up her kitchen. This was incredible. Not only was he charming, sexy, and a good dancer...but he did the dishes? Why. *Why* couldn't he live in Seattle?

Christy finished her dinner and took her plate to the sink, intending to wash it herself, but he shooed her away.

Absolutely amazing. She left him to his moment of domesticity and went to feed her fish. She walked over to the tank and was happy to see her aquatic pet swim to the side to greet her.

"Hello, Fishie!" she crooned softly. "Are you a hungry fish?"

"You named your goldfish Fishie?" Adam asked in bemusement from the kitchen.

"Yeah, I can't figure out if it's a he or she, so I figured *Fishie* was pretty ambiguous."

"Right. How long have you had...er...Fishie?"

"Over a year. I won him at the State Fair."

Adam stopped what he was doing and gave her a look that said he was impressed.

"Well, you must be doing something right. Any fish I ever won at the fair was dead before it even got home."

Christy giggled as she dumped some fish food into the bowl.

Adam wrapped up with the dishes and came to sit down on the futon. He patted the spot next to him and she took a quick breath before going to sit down.

"Take off your heels," he commanded softly.

She blinked. "My heels?"

"Please."

Christy gave him a quick glance, before leaning forward to unfasten the black stilettos. When his hand moved in a light caress down her back, her breath locked in her throat. She kicked off the shoes and raised an eyebrow at him questioningly.

Without responding, he reached down and lifted one of her legs, urging her to sit sideways on the couch so that both of her feet could rest on his lap.

Oh, no, she groaned inwardly. Of course. The perfect man, huh? Here it was, the one big flaw. He had a foot fetish. If he even tried to suck her toes—

"I'm assuming your feet are sore from dancing in those heels all night." He began using his thumbs to massage over the arch of her foot.

"Oh..." The sensation was orgasmic. "You assumed right."

Not a foot-fetish man, just a foot-massaging god! Christy closed her eyes and moaned gratefully as he continued to massage both of her feet.

His fingers slid between her toes and delicious shivers rippled up her spine. He must have realized her reaction, because he looked up from her feet and gave her a slow smile.

"Am I doing this okay?"

"More than okay," she confessed and leaned back against the arm of the futon.

As she sat there, pampered and increasingly aroused, she had a sudden thought. She was in a skirt and her legs were in his lap. What exactly could Adam see? Maybe not enough.

Feeling deliciously wicked, she let her knees fall open and

waited for his response.

Adam swallowed hard, unable to turn his gaze away from the incredible view she'd just given him. Under the black dress, creamy white thighs now lay open with a lacy strip of red between them. Did she realize what she'd just done by changing position?

He jerked his glance up into her face. Oh, yes. Christy knew exactly what she was doing. Well then, game on.

He worked his massage up towards her calf muscles, letting his fingers trail over the sensitive skin behind her knee. She laughed softly and jerked away. There was one ticklish spot revealed.

Hmm. Time to adjust his position. Adam lifted her legs off his lap and came to sit closer to her, folding her knees so her legs were an inverted "V" on the couch. Her dress shifted higher and was nearly at the top of her thighs. He could now see that the red scrap of lace was a tiny thong that left little to the imagination. Blood rushed to his cock and he groaned inwardly.

Adam waited to see if she'd fix the dress, pull it back down, but she made no move towards modesty. Encouraged, he placed his hands just above her knees, pushing them apart. Then he trailed his fingers lightly up and down the tops of her thighs. Her body trembled under the caress.

Needing no further invitation, he angled himself so that he was almost lying between her legs, and then leaned down to kiss her. Her eyes, which had been glazed with arousal, drifted shut as his mouth closed over hers.

Her lips were soft and moist, as she wound her arms around his neck. Her thighs squeezing each side of his hips.

Adam groaned, even through his jeans he could feel the warm heat of her pressing against his growing erection. He reached down and grasped the hem of her dress, pulling it up and over her body. He lifted his head to look down at her and the sight blindsided him. The red lingerie was so sexy it should have been illegal.

He was so caught up in the view that he didn't notice Christy unzipping the fly of his jeans until her fingers were surrounding his cock.

She gasped. "Has anyone ever told you how huge you are?"

The breath hissed out from between his lips, and he didn't bother to answer. Her hand, so soft and small, started moving over him. He eased the jeans down his legs and then went to work taking off her bra. His mouth dried at the sight of her pert, round breasts and the pink puckered nipples.

He kicked off his shoes and socks, and then the pants. She must have been impatient, because she was already pulling his shirt over his head.

"I want to see you naked," she murmured and dragged a short nail down through the trail of curls on his chest. "And I'm liking what I see, cowboy."

"Likewise." He crushed her mouth beneath his again and let his fingers slide between them to the red lace between her legs. "You've soaked through your panties."

Her response was a moan as she grabbed his shoulders and pulled him down to her. He smiled before covering her mouth with his own. He pulled the thin strip of lace between her legs to the side so that her body was open to him.

Adam ran the tips of two fingers over the wet folds of her sex, and breathed in the musky scent of her arousal.

"Damn, you smell good," he muttered against her mouth and then thrust his tongue deep until she parried back with hers.

He worked his fingers just inside her, testing her first, before pushing two to the hilt. She jerked under him, a whimper escaping her lips. She was so hot and wet, snug around his fingers.

The blood pounded in his head, desire making him almost blind.

Christy's hands once again encompassed his dick, and he thought for sure he'd lose it, with the combination of his fingers in her tight pussy, and the feel of her stroking him.

He tore his mouth from hers and kissed the side of her neck, working his way down to her breasts while his fingers continued to stretch and warm her up.

Her nipple teased his mouth, and he licked around the outside before flicking over the distended tip. Finally, he drew it into his mouth and sucked gently on her sweet flesh.

He used his thumb to skim between her legs to find her clitoris. Her hands clenched around his cock in response.

"Christy," he gasped. "You've got to slow down, darlin'."

"I do? You're the one driving me crazy."

She moaned long and loud. He loved the sound. Wanted to hear more of it. He increased the pressure with his thumb, circling her swollen clit until her moans became higher and more strained.

"Adam, oh God, oh...oh my...*God!*"

He knew exactly when she climaxed, her body tightened around him and her eyes slammed shut. The nipple that was in his mouth became even more rigid as her body trembled through the orgasm.

He slowed the pace of his fingers, loving how hot and creamy she'd become.

Finally, when her body went limp, he pulled back. He

searched the floor for his jeans and the condom that was in the pocket. He had it unwrapped and on before she even opened her eyes.

"You sure you're okay with this?" he asked tentatively, stretching her body down the couch so she was lying down. He hooked his fingers on either side of her thong and slid it down and off her body.

"Just shut up and get inside me, cowboy," she whispered, a content smile playing over her face.

"Happy to oblige, ma'am."

He parted her thighs, settled himself between them, and then pushed himself slow and deep inside her. Her slick walls surrounded him, tight and warm. He shut his eyes. *Hello heaven.*

"Oh," she gasped. "I knew you were going to be big."

"Am I hurting you?" he asked, her words penetrating his tunnel vision of sex.

"No, no. It's a good hurt. Like that song."

"Song?" he repeated distractedly.

"You know... *hurts so good, come on baby—*"

"Never mind. Too much talking." He covered her mouth again to quiet her.

He withdrew slightly and then thrust back into her. Her nails drew down his back as their sweaty bodies slid against each other. Increasing his pace, her body jerked beneath him, sliding upward on the couch.

"Yes. Oh God," she gasped. Her hands moved down to grab his ass, pulling him deeper into her.

He leaned down and captured her mouth, thrusting his tongue in to find hers. She was ready for him, meeting each fevered stroke and caress.

Adam felt the tell-tale tightening in his balls and thrust deep two more times before the orgasm ripped through him.

He buried himself to the hilt and groaned into her mouth, all ability to think gone as he shuddered through his climax.

Christy's soft hands moving up and down his back brought him back. The sweet kisses she pressed against his shoulder made him feel oddly possessive of her.

"Thank you." He stroked her hair and kissed her swollen mouth again.

She gave a husky laugh and pulled her mouth away, lowering her lashes. "Mmm. Thank you."

He tucked a strand of hair behind her ear. "Are you tired?"

"Exhausted," she admitted. "It's been a long day."

"Do you have to be anywhere early tomorrow?" he asked.

"Not before noon." She nibbled on her bottom lip. "Is this the part where you leave me?"

"Only if you want me to."

Christy lowered her gaze, taking a moment before shaking her head. "I don't want you to go."

"Then I'll spend the night," he agreed, keeping his voice light. "Under the condition that we make this futon into a bed, and you let me shower in the morning."

"Done deal for both."

He sat up and helped her off the couch before making a quick trip to the bathroom to dispose of the condom. Once he returned, he helped her set the futon up so that it reclined. She pulled a stash of blankets and pillows out from under the frame of the futon and quickly made up the bed.

Adam waited until she crawled under the sheets, and then turned off the lights.

When he climbed in beside her, she rolled close to him. He was surprised that he didn't mind pulling her into his arms. Usually he wasn't big on cuddling, and definitely not on spending the night. So why was it different with Christy? Why was everything different with her?

Not wanting to dwell on that new line of thinking, Adam closed his eyes and tried to fall asleep.

Chapter Four

The sun pouring through the shades convinced Christy to get up. *Mmm. What a night.* She rolled onto her side and glanced at the sleeping man beside her. Had they really fallen asleep cuddling? She never fell asleep in a man's arms. How bizarre. His arm had still been draped across her hip when she'd first woken.

She glanced at the clock on the wall. Yikes, was it already eight-thirty? She climbed off the futon and went to find her cell phone. Nate had promised to call the night before, but she'd turned off her phone. Sure enough, there was a message from him telling her what time they were meeting for lunch. She had a few hours yet.

Christy wrapped a robe around her naked body and walked into the kitchen. She wanted to start breakfast before Adam woke up.

She went to work whipping up pancake batter from scratch. When she was finished, she pulled some frozen blueberries out of the freezer.

She had just measured out a handful to dump into the batter, when she heard Adam enter the kitchen.

"Good morning," she said, without turning around. "I'm just getting ready to make us some break—"

He was behind her, sliding his hands around to the front of her robe. Christy's heart pounded as he undid the loose knot, allowing the robe to fall open. He slid his hands inside to cup each breast.

"I came to say good morning, because I got to thinking about last night," he murmured against her ear. "You have beautiful breasts."

Christy bit back a moan as the blueberries fell from her limp hand into the bowl of pancake batter. He used his thumbs to rub up and down over her nipples. They grew firm and sensitized under his knowing touch.

His hips flexed and this time she did groan as his erection made contact with her lower back.

"Aren't you hungry?" She wished her voice didn't tremble.

"I could eat." One of his hands abandoned a breast and smoothed down her belly to the patch of curls. His fingers toyed there for a moment, before moving confidently down to the folds below. "I could definitely eat."

He penetrated her with one finger and Christy drew in a quick breath, grasping the counter with both hands. She spread her feet apart, allowing him easier access to her body.

He delved deeper before withdrawing his finger and bringing it up to spread the slick moisture over her sensitized clitoris.

Christy groaned. The room spun as his finger ran in circles over her.

His hand left her body abruptly. *No!* She'd been so close to an orgasm. Her body slumped against the counter in disappointment. A second later he picked her up and carried her over to the table.

Christy gripped his shoulders. "What—"

"Shh." He cut off her protest as he knocked a loaf of bread onto the floor, and rolled back the tablecloth. He set her down and then reached back to the counter for the bag of frozen blueberries.

"Frozen?" he asked, raising an eyebrow.

"I haven't had time to pick up any fresh ones." Why was he talking about blueberries after he'd just gotten her all hot and bothered?

"I don't mind." He put one of the frozen berries into his mouth and she could see his tongue running circles over it. *Oh God! Did he have any idea what he was doing to her?*

He pulled the blueberry from his mouth and she was surprised to see it still retained its shape.

"There. Now it's defrosted and ready," he told her, admiring the berry.

"Ready for?" she asked even as he lifted her legs onto the table. He positioned her so that her bottom was on the edge of the table and her legs were spread wide to the edge of each side.

"You're pretty flexible, right? Is this comfortable?"

Huh? For what? "Umm, sure."

He brought the berry between her legs and squeezed it. *Oh!* She inhaled sharply as he began rubbing the juice over her clitoris and into her folds. *Was he going to...? Yes, apparently he was!*

Adam sank down onto his knees and she held her breath.

His tongue, wet and textured, drew bluntly over her clit to lick up the juices.

"Oh God," she gasped, her bottom clenching. He licked her again, sweeping his tongue up her cleft to flick over the bud again.

His murmur of approval sent a heated flush through her,

just before he drew her clit into his mouth and started sucking.

She groaned, loud and guttural, watching his mouth move on her. He brought up two fingers to thrust deep inside her and she screamed. She gripped the table to keep from falling backwards.

When the orgasm started to roll over her, she didn't fight it. Instead, she lifted her hips against his mouth and fingers, clenching around him as waves of intense pleasure rolled over her. Then she did fall back on the table and away from Adam's skilled mouth and hand.

He stood up with a soft laugh, letting his fingers trail over her quivering stomach. He pulled the edges of her robe together and tied the knot firmly back in place.

"I don't know if I mentioned it, but I love blueberries."

Christy managed a strangled laugh as she opened her eyes. The smile she gave him was weak, but then so were her words.

"Can I just say how that was a really fantastic way to start the morning?"

"I couldn't agree more. Now, did I hear something about breakfast?"

"Breakfast? Don't you want to make a side trip to the futon?" she asked, glancing at the crotch of his jeans.

"More than anything." He leaned down and kissed the side of her neck. "But unless you have any condoms, I'm all out."

Christy sighed. *How disappointing.* "I wish I had one. But before last night I hadn't had sex in two years. Condoms aren't exactly something I keep on hand."

There was a pause. "I'm honored."

"That I don't have condoms?"

"That I'm your first in two years," he replied, seeming almost astonished.

"Don't be. It's not much of an honor, really." Christy averted her gaze. *God, now this was just embarrassing.* She shouldn't have admitted her lack of a sex life to him. "I should get started on the pancakes. Did you want to take that shower while I'm cooking?"

"I think I will, darlin'. Thanks," he replied, and helped her off the table.

He was such a gentleman. She watched his firm butt disappear into the bathroom. What a man. He was impressive in and out of the bedroom. Not to mention the kitchen table. He seemed like the perfect candidate to break her crappy men streak. Then again, he wouldn't be around long enough.

"I can't think about this now," Christy muttered, and went to finish cooking them breakfast.

She cooked herself one pancake and ate it while making his to save time. By the time she'd finished preparing his breakfast and had set it out on the table for him, Adam was coming out of the bathroom. She swallowed another wave of disappointment that they didn't have another condom. He looked positively sinful with his wet hair still dripping onto his hard, muscled chest.

"Help yourself to whatever you want," she offered and set a bottle of syrup on the table beside the butter. "There's a pot of coffee on the counter if you want some. Don't worry, it's not that *fancy espresso stuff.*"

Adam had already sat down, drenched his pancakes in syrup, and taken a bite before she'd finished talking. This man was the epitome of a man's man.

Time for her shower now. She went to move past him, but he caught her hand. She didn't resist as he pulled her down onto his lap.

"Thank you for breakfast." He lowered his head to kiss her.

He tasted of syrup, as his tongue stroked slowly against hers. Sweet and tempting. She let herself enjoy a few more seconds of the sensual kiss, before drawing back reluctantly.

"I really need to shower. I smell like I just spent the night having wild and kinky sex."

Adam smiled and drawled, "You did spend the night having wild and kinky sex."

"Yes, and that's why I'm going to shower now. I'll be out soon."

"Have some of your pancakes first," he urged, stabbing a bite with his fork and holding it to her mouth.

"I had one already."

"Bah. One is nothing. Have more."

She sighed and leaned forward, wrapping her lips around the fork. Pulling the pancake off into her mouth, she chewed and then swallowed.

"How is it?"

"Mmm, I'm a good cook."

Adam laughed and fed her another bite. And then another. She stayed snuggled on his lap until she'd eaten one of his five pancakes. Finally, she scooted off him.

"I really need to get that shower."

"All right, darlin', I'll see you when you're done."

Christy blew him a kiss and then walked into the bathroom, shutting the door behind her. She leaned against the frame for a moment, a giddy smile across her face. The last twelve hours had seemed surreal. Had she ever been this happy with a guy?

A cell phone rang, and she listened to make sure it wasn't hers. Nope, it was his. She heard him answer a second later. Christy turned on the shower, and then slipped out of her robe and stepped under the warm spray.

When she came out of the bathroom twenty minutes later, it was clear that Adam was gone. She tightened the towel around her body. Oh God. See, he wasn't perfect. It had only been about sex. Oh, and that cute little pancake feeding scene? Just a way to throw her off so he could escape the moment she got in the shower. She'd never see him again. *Stop panicking, Christy, calm down!* Oh God...

She noticed the note sitting on the table by his empty plate. Biting her lip, she hurried over to it. Here it was. The moment of truth. Would it be a good note, or bad note? She scanned it.

God, she was such a dork. Of course he hadn't ditched her like last week's leftovers. The phone call had been important, and he'd had to leave immediately. And he'd signed it saying he'd see her at dance class later on.

Christy set the note back on the table and glanced at the clock on the wall. That was nine hours away. Well, at least now she knew how she'd spend part of the time. Buying the biggest box of condoms she could find.

Wait. There was still lunch. Oh yeah. She had to meet Nate's family. There it was again, that stab of discomfort. This seemed like such a bad idea. But she'd promised, and she couldn't just go back on her word.

Jeez. And what the heck did someone wear when they were going to meet an ultra-conservative family? Hmm. Maybe she had a turtleneck somewhere in her closet.

Christy glanced over at Nate as he drove them to the restaurant. His face was pale, and his palms looked sweaty as they gripped the steering wheel.

"You're a good actress, right?" he asked for the third time since he'd picked her up. "You can make this believable, right?"

"Will you relax, Nate?" She sighed and shook her head. "I'm great with parents. They'll love me, I promise. You should be more worried about yourself and how you're going to convince them."

"I'll be all right. Brian's been giving me some pointers and lessons on how to pull this off."

"Are you serious?" She figured Brian must be the drama major Nate had talked about yesterday. God, was that only yesterday? It was amazing what could happen in twenty-four hours.

"Everyone will believe I'm your lover," he promised. "You look great by the way. I like your outfit, not too sexy, but still feminine enough for my mom to adore you."

"Thanks." God. His parents sounded weirder by the minute. She was glad she'd picked the khakis and lavender sweater set.

Nate steered his car into a parking spot at the restaurant and gave her another sharp glance.

"Are you ready for this?"

She really wanted to say no and give him an earful. But instead she gave a curt nod.

They left the car and strolled into the restaurant, Nate's arm draped casually around her waist.

He gave the hostess his name and was led over to a table where an older couple was seated.

Christy looked them over with a curious glance. So these were the parents, hmm?

His father was tall with dark hair, and dark eyes. The woman seated was gently rounded and looked to be in her early fifties; highlighted blonde hair and eyes that sparkled with curiosity as she watched her son approach. Not a bad-looking couple overall. She certainly wasn't getting the *American Gothic* vibe Nate had portrayed.

"Nate." His mother stood up and hurried around the table to give him a hug. "Oh, honey, it's been so long! And you must be Christy."

Christy found herself pulled into Nate's mother's arms. She returned the hug, feeling like the biggest fake in the world. This was so wrong.

Nate stepped back with a slight laugh. "Christy, I'd like you to meet my mom, Candace, and my dad, Steven."

"Christy, it's good to finally meet you," Candace exclaimed and clutched Christy's hands. Her gaze scanned her almost skeptically. "Nate's been telling us all about you for the past three months, and I just knew you had to be special."

Christy almost didn't hear her. She was focused on Candace's eyes, they seemed somewhat familiar. Then her words registered and she gave Nate a sharp glance.

Three months? He'd had this planned for three months? He hadn't even asked her to pose for this charade until yesterday. Ugh! When they got out of here, he was going to get it.

"I've heard a lot about you both, too," she replied politely, giving them a warm smile. "I'm so glad we could all finally have lunch together."

"Us as well." Steven cleared his throat and gestured for them all to sit. He turned to Nate. "Your brother is running a little late. But he said he'd join us as soon as possible."

"He's running late? Now there's a surprise." Nate draped an arm around the back of Christy's chair, giving her a smile that in all appearances was intimate and loving.

Now's your Hollywood moment, she told herself. *Get those acting genes out of the basement.* She returned his smile with even more brilliance, even batted her eyelashes a bit.

"Be nice, sweetie. He's your brother," she chided and gave him a gentle nudge.

Nate shrugged. "You're always so good at reminding me when I'm out of line. Thanks, honey."

"No problem, what are girlfriends and wives for if not to keep their boyfriends and husbands in line?" she teased and sent a conspiring glance to Candace. Thatta girl, build the camaraderie with the mom.

Candace's brows drew into a frown, before she laughed and picked up the menu to look it over. Hmm. Maybe the parents weren't too keen on her after all.

Christy glanced down at her own menu, vowing to step it up a little.

"So, when did you guys arrive?" Nate asked his parents.

"We got into town last night," Steven answered. "But Adam arrived on Sunday evening, I believe. Said he had some business in the city he'd like to take care of."

Christy looked up at the mention of the name Adam. Memories of last night flooded through her body and she tingled at the images in her head.

She leaned towards Nate and whispered in his ear, "How ironic, the guy I brought home last night is named Adam. Wouldn't it be funny if he was your brother? God. That would be a mess."

Nate's eyebrow rose with interest and he kept his voice quiet as he replied, "Coffee shop guy? You'd better tell me details later. And don't worry. My brother would never take Salsa lessons. He's your typical alpha male."

"What are you kids whispering about over there?" Candace

asked, setting down her menu. "You look like such a...happy couple."

It sounded odd the way she'd said it, Christy thought, her smile wobbling a bit.

Nate lifted her hand and kissed her knuckles. "Well, she's just so adorable, aren't you, honey? I couldn't help falling for you."

Step it up, remember? Christy sighed and lowered her lashes. "Sweetie, you're making me blush. The truth is, Candace, your son is so charming I fell in love with him ten minutes after I met him."

Candace's brows shot up.

"Is that so?" A voice drawled from behind her. "And which son is that?"

No. No! All the hairs on the back of Christy's neck stood up. She continued to stare at Candace's eyes. Now she knew why they were so familiar. Just like she knew exactly who'd be behind her when she turned around. No... Oh, please... No.

Forget her statement to Nate a moment ago. This was definitely not funny. But it was about to be a big mess.

Chapter Five

Christy turned slowly in her seat and reluctantly raised her gaze.

Adam stood towering over them, with a lopsided smile on his face, but the eyes that stared down at her were filled with silent accusations. She flinched and her stomach rolled.

"Adam," Candace scolded her son with mock disapproval. "Now don't you go flirting with your brother's girlfriend. You're going to scare the poor girl off."

"I wouldn't want to do that," Adam replied and walked around to kiss him mom on the cheek. "She seems like such a *decent* girl."

It's not what you think! Christy wanted to scream. She gave Nate a furtive glance, but he had turned to sulking into his menu since Adam's arrival. She dropped her gaze. There had to be a way out of this situation. There had to!

She'd talk to Nate on the drive home. Explain that she couldn't do this anymore and he'd have to fess up. There was no way, *no way* she was going to risk whatever she had with Adam. Not for this—a fake charade to cover Nate's profuse gayness.

"How long have you two been together, anyway?" Adam asked, his question seemingly innocent to everyone else.

Christy knew better. He was digging, he wanted answers. Probably putting together an erroneous puzzle in his head.

She had to say something. "We're actually—"

"What is it, a year now?" Nate cut in, giving her leg a swift warning kick under the table. "I only mentioned you to Mom and Dad a few months ago. I knew we were trying to keep things quiet."

What? Christy retaliated and kicked him back harder. How dare he? Nate didn't even flinch or glance her way.

"Is that so? One year?" Adam whistled and picked up his menu. Christy noted his knuckles were white from grasping it so hard. "That seems like a real long time for two people to stay in a monogamous relationship. Don't you find it *hard*, Christy?"

"Not really, Adam," Nate answered for her. Giving his brother a smile that was more bitter than friendly. "We don't all go through more women in a week than there are days. I wonder if you'll ever change."

Christy stiffened. More women in a week...?

"Why? What can I say?" Adam turned his gaze back to Christy. "Apparently the ladies like me."

The blood drained from her face as she stared at him. Who was this guy? What had happened to her sweet, sexy cowboy? *God, I'm a fool.* She'd slept with Adam two days after meeting him. She didn't know squat about him.

Christy lowered her gaze. God, she felt sick.

"Gentlemen." Their father's voice turned harsh. "That is quite enough. We are at a nice restaurant, and you could at least try to be civil to each other."

"You're right, Dad," Adam murmured. "And I apologize if I crossed the line."

Candace was looking around the table, obviously upset and

confused at the turn of atmosphere.

The waitress came to the table just then and stopped the tension from increasing. Christy rambled off the first thing she saw on the menu. Then the waitress turned to face Adam.

"And you, sir?"

"I'll just have a slice of pie. I had a late breakfast." He turned his smile away from the waitress and directed it at Christy. "You wouldn't happen to have blueberry, would you?"

Christy's face flamed. Oh God. She had to get away from the table before she lost it.

"Excuse me," she forced herself to say through numb lips. "I need to use the restroom."

She pushed back her chair, tossed her napkin on the table, and practically ran from the room.

Adam watched her go, trying to control the furious tic in his jaw. Well, hell.

What kind of game had she been playing? Christy was Nate's girlfriend? Women had always flirted with Nate, but he'd never settled down. What made Christy so different? And had she known who Adam was when she'd taken him to her bed last night? Doubtful, judging by her horrified reaction.

"Is she sick?" their mom asked, her expression worried. Then a smile flitted across her face, almost amusement. "She couldn't be pregnant. Could she?"

"*Mother.*" Nate sounded shocked.

Adam's hand clenched around his water glass so tight, he was surprised it didn't snap in half.

Damn, he was fool. He'd been lying in bed with her last night already thinking that she could be The One. Thinking how sweet and innocent she was.

Right, innocent like a barracuda.

"Don't you think you should go check on her?" their mom asked.

Nate turned his gaze away from the window and shrugged. "I'm sure she's fine."

Adam's eyes narrowed. Kind of an indifferent attitude to take with a girlfriend. He glanced towards the restrooms and saw Christy emerge. She still looked shell-shocked, and seemed like she'd rather bolt than return to their table.

But she did return, sitting back down and not meeting his questioning gaze. Why wouldn't she look at him? Couldn't handle the guilt? She picked up her glass of water and took a tiny sip.

"Are you feeling all right, dear?" their mom asked her. "Can we get you some tea?"

"I'm fine. Thank you, Mrs. Young."

"Please, call me Candace, dear."

Christy's responding smile was wan. "All right, Candace."

"Did you wrap up your business this morning, Adam?" his father asked.

"Most of it." He kept his gaze on Christy. "But I think there's still another thing I've got to see to."

She flushed but still didn't look up.

"It's all business and no pleasure for you." His mom shook her head. "We came to Seattle for a vacation, Adam. And I so hoped you might use the time to relax."

"It hasn't all been business." He turned his attention back to his mom. "Don't you worry, Mother. I always manage to squeeze in some pleasure."

Out of the corner of his eye he saw Christy flinch. Damn, maybe he shouldn't have said that. Being an asshole wasn't going to solve anything.

"So, Adam," Christy began, her voice sounding perfectly calm now. She must be a damn good actress. "I'm a little confused. Nate told me you ran a little fruit business, but I also heard you were a firefighter. Which one is it?"

"Little fruit business?" His mom laughed. "It may have started little, but Adam's Apples and Cider has become quite large, especially over in Eastern Washington."

"You're Adam from Adam's Apples?" Christy repeated, looking like she'd just taken another hit.

"That's me, darlin'." The "darlin'" came out before he could remember to check it. Hopefully his mom wouldn't call him on flirting again. "And you heard right, I'm also a volunteer firefighter."

Her chin lifted and her mouth tightened. "Well, you certainly keep yourself busy."

The trembling in her hands was so small, he was probably the only one who noticed the ice in her glass shaking.

"So, you've heard of us?" his dad asked, looking proud. "I love it when folks from the city have heard of Adam's business. He worked darn hard to build that thing up."

"I have, yes." Christy glanced at Nate, who hadn't said a word in about ten minutes. "Although, Nate never mentioned it by name."

"He never mentioned the business?" Adam bit back a sigh, wondering why the hell it bugged him so much. Nate had never acknowledged his success—seemed to resent it. It irked. They'd been so close once. "Did he mention that he had a brother?"

"He mentioned you," Christy said curtly, but still didn't meet his gaze.

Nate finally looked up with a shrug. "Maybe I didn't want to deal with the competition. It wouldn't be the first time a woman chose you over me."

Adam didn't respond for a moment. Was Nate referring to Jenny Wilson? Shoot. That had been in the seventh grade. *Seventh grade*. He wouldn't hold a grudge that long, would he?

Well, at least Nate had no clue about what had happened between him and Christy last night. That would really push him over the edge. Rightfully so. Disappointment clenched his gut. What had she been thinking last night?

Lunch arrived and conversation dwindled to a halt. His parents looked a little uncomfortable as they started in on their burgers. Christy picked up a chicken strip, glared at it, and then set it back down.

Only Nate seemed to be enjoying his lunch—some kind of salad packed with veggies, and devoid of anything that had ever walked the earth.

Adam glanced down at his own slice of blueberry pie. What the hell had he been thinking ordering it? The sight of it pissed him off and—truth be told—made him a little depressed.

He set it aside and glanced out the window. Now would be a good time to have a cigarette. Too bad he'd quit smoking five years ago.

Christy couldn't have been happier to see the check when it arrived. She needed to get out of here. Now. Adam insisted on paying, and Nate made no move to protest. Which was odd, usually Nate was more than ready to pick up the tab if not pay his own share.

"It was nice meeting you," she said honestly to his parents. They spent a moment telling her how great she was and setting up a dinner for Saturday, before leaving the restaurant to find some more tourist attractions to see.

Because good etiquette dictated that she also say goodbye to Adam, she turned to face him. What the hell was she going to say? *Thanks for the sex last night, and please just ignore this whole deal about me being Nate's girlfriend. It's all just an act.*

"Do you want some money?" she offered.

Adam's head reared up from the credit card copy he was signing and his eyes narrowed.

"For lunch," she added quickly. It didn't take a genius to figure out he'd interpreted the comment to be something more sinister.

"I don't need your money, Christy." His smile was so hard that she flinched. His gaze lifted to someone behind her, and she glanced back to see that Nate had stepped back within earshot.

"Are you ready, honey?" he asked and wrapped an arm around her waist.

I'm going to cry. The thought came on so suddenly, she had to blink rapidly before she dropped her gaze. "Yes, I'm ready. Thank you for lunch, Adam."

She turned and left with Nate, not waiting for his response.

When they were pulling out of the parking lot, only then did she let out a pained groan.

"Do you realize what just happened in there?"

"What, that you slept with my brother last night?" he replied with a snort. "Yeah, I figured that out pretty quick. You looked like you were going to throw up, and Adam looked like he wanted to throw knives."

"You *knew*? And you did nothing?" Her eyes widened and annoyance nipped at her. "Don't you see? We have to call this off. I really like your brother, Nate. Last night was—"

"Sex, Christy," he cut her off. "And I'm not going to let you consider for a moment that it was more than that. You don't know Adam like I do. The man loves women. Like *loves* them. I guarantee you, last night was just about getting laid for him."

The blood drained from her face and she swallowed hard. "That's a little harsh."

"And it's a lot true." Nate sighed and grabbed her hand. "Honey, I'm trying to help you understand here. He was never going to call you after last night."

She shook her head, struggling to push aside the sudden doubt. "What? He said he would. And he slept at my place."

Nate gave her a disbelieving look and then frowned when he realized that she was serious. "That's a little unusual for him, but I don't think it changes anything."

"Meaning?"

"Meaning him getting you into bed was just another one of his goals. Women and work are his hobbies. Most women don't hold out sex for more than a few hours with him, let alone two days. So don't feel bad."

"Don't feel bad?" she repeated, her voice rising. "You're telling me not to feel bad after I just had the most amazing night of my life. Don't feel bad that the man I just slept with is the rich, powerful, entrepreneur brother of my best friend? And apparently to him I was just another notch on the bedpost. Is that it?"

"It's a pretty good sum. Nice how you threw in the powerful and rich part."

Christy was too busy with her own hurt to acknowledge the bitterness behind his words.

"Are you just telling me this because you're afraid I'll insist that we quit this stupid charade?"

"No. I'm telling you this because I care about you. If I had known it was my brother Adam you'd met at the coffee shop, I would never have encouraged you to pursue it."

"And that's it?"

"Yes."

"Bullshit." She shook her head. "You'd say anything to convince me to go along with this ridiculous pretense."

Nate's hands clenched around the steering wheel. "Listen, Christy—"

"You listen. You're being a selfish ass, Nate." All of a sudden it was too much. "Stop the car."

"What?" He glanced at her in alarm.

"Stop the freaking car before I jump out!"

He hit the brakes and the car jerked to a stop, flinging her forward against the seatbelt. She fumbled with the fastening, and then reached for the door handle.

Nate grabbed her arm. "You can't just walk home, Christy."

Her eyes narrowed. "You had me thinking Adam ran some little fruit stand on the side of the road."

He hesitated. "I misled you. I'm sorry."

"You also made him out to be some dumb, massive hick from the country."

"Well, he kind of is..."

She gave him a look of disbelief.

"*Fine.* I got my mom's short height and dad's dark features. Adam's the perfect, tall golden boy." He scowled. "Happy now?"

"Uh, no. I am so far from happy right now, Nate." She shook her head. "You keep lying to me. Everything you've said so far has been a lie. Why should I believe anything you've told me today about Adam?"

"Because you're my best friend."

Christy climbed out of the car. "You're going to have to do better than that."

He rolled down his window, moving the car alongside her as she hurried down the street. "You're not going to walk home, Christy."

"Wanna bet?"

Nate cursed, and then hit the gas and drove off.

Of all the... Christy stared after him in disbelief. He'd actually left her.

He was damn lucky that she didn't have Adam's cell phone number. Otherwise she'd be dialing him up to have a long talk right about now.

Chapter Six

Christy sat on the futon, a carton of ice cream on her lap, and a Women's Network movie playing on the television. Usually she wasn't big on the sad, depressing chick movies. But today it was comforting to see people with crappier luck than hers.

She jammed her spoon back into the chocolate ice cream. It could have been worse. She could've been the woman in the movie. Finding out that her sixteen-year-old daughter was sleeping with her fiancé.

Christy tucked her legs under her feet. She'd really gone into *poor me* mode. Not only was she delving into the ice cream and dismal television, she'd also thrown on the sweats. But damn if her legs and feet didn't hurt from that long walk home.

Stupid Nate. God, she was still pissed at him.

At least class didn't start for another three hours. And she planned on spending those three hours feeling sorry for herself and for the woman in the movie.

The knock on her door finally jerked Christy from a trancelike state. She looked away from the television with a frown, then set down the half-empty ice cream and went to the door.

She leaned forward to look through the peephole, then jerked back in surprise. Uh-oh. She hadn't seen this coming.

Although she probably should have.

She slowly tiptoed backwards, deciding it would be better to pretend she wasn't there.

"I saw your eye against the peephole, Christy," Adam called out.

She grunted in disbelief and made a face at the door. Maybe he'd give up and leave.

"I'm not going away until we talk."

So much for that idea.

"I'm not dressed," she lied, and then wished she'd picked a less visual excuse when he didn't respond right away.

Finally he said, "I'll wait while you put your clothes on."

God he was persistent. She sighed and unlocked the door, flinging it open to face him.

"I thought you weren't dressed?" He stepped past her and into the apartment, shutting the door firmly behind him.

Christy shrugged and folded her arms across her chest as she stared at him. Her chest was tight, and her throat ached with the urge to try to explain.

She wanted to. Had threatened Nate that she would. But did Adam want an explanation? Was that why he was here? Or was he just going to berate her? Hell, she deserved it.

She waited for him to say something more, but he just continued to walk around her apartment in silence.

"I'm a little surprised to see you here," she finally said. "I didn't think you'd want to have anything to do with me after..." He stopped, turning to face her as she trailed off. "After this morning."

Adam tilted his head. "What makes you think I want anything to do with you?"

Ouch. She swallowed hard. "You're here."

"So I am." He walked over to her futon and sat down, lifting up the carton of ice cream. "I came to hear what you had to say."

Ah. So he did want an explanation. Now was her moment. She took a deep breath.

"I'm not really..." She faltered and bit her lip. Say it! "Nate doesn't..."

She closed her eyes.

God. She couldn't do it. Maybe Nate was completely out of line, but she didn't have the right to do this to him. To out him like this.

"Nate doesn't what, Christy?"

She opened her eyes again and shook her head. "Never mind."

Adam picked up the spoon and took a bite of her ice cream. Oh God. Her eyes narrowed on his mouth. That was so erotic. Watching him lick the spoon that she'd so recently had her lips wrapped around. Was she drooling? Christy shut her mouth.

"Last night," he murmured. "Things got pretty intimate between us. Don't you agree, darlin'?"

"I—you could say so." Those lips. That tongue. Intimate was an understatement.

"I would most definitely say so." He scooped another spoonful of ice cream into his mouth.

Her heart raced as she watched him sitting on her futon, licking her spoon. This morning he'd been licking other things.

She shook her head. *Get a grip, horny.* "I'm sorry, what were you saying?"

What was he doing here, anyway? Any other man probably would have taken a good look at his situation and written her off as a two-timing bitch slut. A good conclusion, if her situation had been legit.

Adam set the ice cream back down and looked up at her. "I was just thinking that you probably had your side of the story."

"My side of the story?" she repeated. Oh, Lord. He was still giving her a chance to redeem herself. A way to explain her way out of it? Why? Why did he care so much? If he was the type of guy Nate said he was, he should be happy he'd been given an easy out.

"You must have had your reasons for going to bed with me when you already had a boyfriend."

"Oh, that." Her laugh tinkled artificially. What the hell did she say?

"Yes, that."

Christy looked at him, really looked at him. Despite his light tone and casual demeanor, he was seriously pissed off.

Say something. *Anything.* "Umm...well, it's exactly how it looks. It was just casual sex between us. There is no explanation."

Adam's gaze narrowed. There was a long pause.

"I don't buy it."

Christy blinked in surprise. What more could he want? "You don't? Why not?"

"Because you didn't act like a woman who was thinking about a one-night stand."

God, he could he read her that well? "I didn't?"

"No. You didn't." He took a step towards her. "You acted like a woman who was falling hard."

"You're pretty cocky there, cowboy." Damn it. He wasn't supposed to argue with her about this. Even if he was right. He was supposed to get really pissed off and leave.

"You're not the first to tell me that." He touched a strand of her hair, rubbing it between his fingers. "Are you pregnant?"

"What?" Christy yelped, her blood pounding. "We used protection last night. I shouldn't be."

"Not with me."

"Not you? Then—" She broke off, wanting to smash her head into the wall. Nate. Hello. Could she possibly screw this up anymore?

Adam had done nothing but turn her brain to mush the past couple of days. And now he was looking at her like she must be out of her mind. And she was.

An idea hit her. A lie that was kind of funny, and kind of payback to Nate. If she was going to lie to Adam, it was going to be on her terms.

She heaved a dramatic *okay you win* sigh. "Fine, you want to know the truth?"

"Yes."

"Nate and I haven't had sex." Perfect, no lie there. "He has an erectile dysfunction problem."

Adam stared at her, a look of disbelief and horror on his face. Why did he look so shocked? Was he worried it ran in the family or something?

He hesitated. "Are you saying that Nate can't..."

Christy nodded solemnly. "Get it up. That's exactly what I'm saying."

Adam looked away and she heard the breath hiss out from between his teeth.

"You're saying you've never had sex with Nate?"

"Never." Yes! Another non-lie.

"But..." Adam looked absolutely perplexed. "Why would you

stay with a man you can't have sex with?"

"Because...there's always hope. He's seeking help." Oh God, could that sound anymore cheesy? Christy touched his arm. "He's a good guy, Adam, and there's more to a relationship than sex."

"Sure, but sex is a big part of it."

Spoken like a true man.

Adam stared at her and then his eyes narrowed. "Why do I get the feeling you're hiding something?"

Because I am. Jeez. He didn't give up. He was like a dog with a bone.

Adam stepped towards her, and she took a nervous step back. They repeated the process until she was right against the wall. Then he lifted a finger and trailed it over her collarbone.

He was touching her. Not good. So not good. Goosebumps broke out over her flesh, and a tremor swept through her body.

"Why did you offer me money this afternoon? Were you trying to buy my silence?"

"Buy your silence?"

"About what happened between us." His finger drifted lower until it traced across the top of her breast. "Are you afraid I'll go to Nate and explain to him what happened last night?"

Hell, she wished he *would* go to Nate. Then maybe it would force a break up between them. But she couldn't exactly say that.

"I don't know." It was the only response she had.

"Then answer the other question. Were you trying to buy my silence?"

"No. That's ridiculous." At least that was an honest answer. "I was trying to buy my lunch."

His laughter was soft. "Tell me, Christy. What would you do for me to ensure that I kept quiet?"

Whoa. Hold on a minute. Was he...? Damn, he was. There was a definite innuendo there, dripping with sexual undertones. He slipped his finger lower on her breast.

"Adam..." She gasped. If he continued doing what he was doing, she was going to completely blow her act. And then Adam.

"What would you do, Christy?" he whispered, his mouth just inches above hers.

Her eyes shut. God, she just wanted his mouth on hers. Why wasn't there some kind of loophole to the whole promise thing? Wait a minute. Maybe there was.

All of a sudden she had a beautiful plan. Adam was pretty much trying to blackmail her into having sex with him, right? So why didn't she just give in? It was the perfect loophole. Kind of a dark loophole, but it worked.

It did put Adam in kind of a bad light, though. Honestly, what kind of man would blackmail his brother's girlfriend into having sex with him? Ah, hell, she didn't want to think about that right now.

She glanced up at him from under her lashes and said, "I'll do whatever you want me to do, cowboy."

Adam's indrawn breath was sharp. He hesitated before jerking away from her so fast that she fell back against the wall.

"Yeah, I about figured as much."

Umm. Okay. Not exactly the response she'd hoped for. He'd been testing her? So wait, what did this mean?

"Uh, wait," she called after him. "Are you going to tell Nate about us?"

He gave her a disgusted look before striding out her front

door and letting it slam shut behind him.

Great. Nice going, Christy. She slid down the wall and sat on the ground. So not only did he turn out to be a decent guy, but she'd just made herself look like a complete whore.

☙

Christy arrived at Salsa class that night and glanced around. Was Adam going to show? Common sense kicked in. Not a chance. The man was pissed. Rightfully so.

And even if there hadn't been the whole drama with pretending to be Nate's girlfriend, Adam had already slept with her. There was no reason for him to keep torturing himself with dance lessons.

Carlos entered the building while she was stretching. "Bad day, *niña*?"

She was scowling and hadn't even realized it. Glancing up at him, she offered a brief shrug in return. "I'm sure I've had worse. I just really can't remember one right now."

Carlos gave her a sympathetic smile and went to turn on the music.

"He will not show up tonight then?"

"Let's just say that I would be very surprised if he did," she muttered. "And now I'm getting a raging headache. Do you have anything?"

"Sorry, I don't do drugs."

"Drugs? It's like taking a breath mint." Christy rolled her eyes. "You don't know what you're missing."

Despite her headache, she managed to get through class. And like she'd predicted, Adam didn't show.

What, Christy, you actually deluded yourself into thinking otherwise? She shook her head and locked up before heading out to her car.

Nate's family said they were leaving on Sunday. Four days from now. She was having dinner with them on Saturday, but that was it. Only a couple more hours of pulling the wool over their eyes. And over Adam's.

Although he hadn't seemed entirely convinced earlier today. He seemed like a pretty sharp guy who didn't miss much. Fooling Adam was, and still would be, the hard part. Mostly because it made her so depressed to think about what she was sacrificing.

Maybe, when this was all over, she would try to talk to Adam and see if they could give it another go. God. That was an absurd thought.

Relationships had to have trust, and right off the bat she'd blown that with him.

She sighed. *Let him go, Christy, let him go.*

ଔ

Adam sat in the leather recliner in his room, staring out at Elliot Bay. He tilted a bottle of beer back towards his mouth and took a hard swig.

The thing was, usually he wouldn't have taken it so hard. The whole Christy and Nate thing.

He was used to dating women on a casual basis, and Christy wasn't the first one who'd turned out to have a boyfriend. Or husband for that matter. Though sleeping with a woman who was already spoken for wasn't his usual practice. There were enough available ones to suit his needs.

But in the cases where it did happen, he ended things right away. Closed that book and moved on. So why should this time be any different?

But it was. Painfully different. He couldn't stop thinking about Christy's sunny smile and sinfully tempting curves. The way her eyes sparkled with an invitation and then grew wide when she realized she might have bitten off more than she could chew.

He tried to picture her giving those same looks to his brother, and he couldn't bring up the image. Or maybe he just didn't want to.

And then there was that conversation they'd had after he'd been stupid enough to show up at her apartment. The way she'd pretty much offered herself to him in exchange for his silence. And Lord if he hadn't been tempted. But he was above that. She was above that. At least he'd pegged her to be. So what the hell was going on?

He stood up and paced over to the fridge to grab another beer. Walking back to the window, Adam watched the wind whip the waves of Puget Sound into a frenzy.

There was something weird about the whole Christy and Nate thing. And he wanted to figure out what. He wanted to know everything about Christy…not just where he could kiss her to make her squirm.

Yes, he wanted to know everything about her. Including how serious her relationship with Nate was.

Adam picked up the phone and dialed his brother.

ঞ

"Christy? It's Nate."

Christy took a bite of her Caesar salad and shifted the phone closer to her ear.

"So I noticed. What can I do for you?"

"Thank you for not saying anything to Adam about us. About me."

"What makes you think I didn't?" She decided not to fill him in on the erectile dysfunction lie.

"Well, he just called me, but didn't say anything about it."

Christy immediately sat up straighter on her futon. "Oh. What *did* he say? Did he confront you about our night together?" *Did she sound too eager?*

"No. Why? Did he say he was going to?"

Bummer. Big bummer. "Not exactly. Anyway, what did he say then?"

"He wants us to meet him and my parents down on the waterfront in an hour."

See Adam again? No. She wouldn't do it. "Why?"

"He wants us to escort him on some of the big Seattle attractions."

"Oh does he now? Do I look like I have the words *Tourist Guide* stamped on my forehead? If he wants to act like a tourist, he can Ride the Duck with everyone else. Hell, I hear that's a great family tour."

"Christy, you don't work until tonight. You could do it."

"And what if I have plans today?" she demanded. "Come on, Nate. This wasn't part of the deal. It was lunch yesterday and dinner on Saturday. No tourism Thursday included."

"Do you have plans?"

It was on the tip of her tongue to tell him yes. "No. But that doesn't mean I want to chaperone your brother on a freaking field trip. Why can't you do it?"

"I am doing it. I've had plans to spend today with them for a while now. Adam called me this morning and requested that I bring you."

Her heart sped up. Why did he want her to come? It would just end badly again. "Here's what you tell him to do with that request—"

"*Christy.*"

She sighed. "Tell him I'm busy."

"Look. Adam has done a lot for me," Nate admitted, his tone hesitant. "I may not get along with him that well, but he's bailed me out financially more than once this past year."

"And that's my problem how?"

"I owe him, Christy. And he wants you to come today. You must have really got him interested."

Her pulse jumped again.

"Christy, maybe I was wrong. Maybe Adam really did feel differently about you."

"What are you getting at here, Nate?"

"Well, maybe after this week is up, you guys could give it a shot together."

"What?" Christy dropped her fork into her salad. "Are you kidding me? After you telling me what a bad idea it was? How he—"

"Look, I have never seen Adam get all twittery like this over a woman. He brings you up every time I talk to him."

"Really?" Her voice squeaked with hope. *God she was pathetic.*

"Really. And that's why I want you to come today. Get to know Adam better—outside the bedroom. See what you think of him when you're not being ruled by your hormones. Besides, would it kill you to do the tourist scene for a couple of hours?"

"No." Her stomach twisted. "It would kill me to keep up this charade in front of the man I'm falling for."

Nate groaned on the other end of the phone.

"Why is he doing this?" she asked. "Why can't he be like a normal guy and just ignore me?"

"Because he's not normal, he's Adam and he's nowhere near ready to ignore you. Sorry, darling."

"Don't call me that," she muttered. "Adam calls me that, but with more of a country twang."

"Darlin'?"

"There you go."

"So will you do it?"

She was so weak, but God she really did want to see Adam again. Christy closed her eyes. "I guess so. God, I'm such a pushover. Anyone else would have told you to go to hell two favors ago."

"That's why I love you, and I will so redeem myself after this. I promise."

"So when and where on the waterfront?"

"One at the aquarium. Do you want me to pick you up?"

"No. I'll meet you there." She hung up the phone.

Great, now she actually had to take a shower. If she had to meet him, she wanted to look good doing it.

Christy stood on the sidewalk of the waterfront, leaning against the stone railing as she watched the ferries pulling into Elliot Bay.

The weather was warm for Seattle—the mid-seventies—and

she was glad with the outfit she'd chosen. Not to mention it was just plain old cute—white bohemian-style skirt, and a pink tank top. And the beaded sandals just made the outfit.

She glanced at her watch. Had she heard the time wrong from Nate? Or was everyone just running late?

"You look worried."

Christy pushed aside the tummy butterflies, and turned around to give Adam her blandest smile. At least she hoped it was bland, because her pulse had just gone into double time.

"Not worried. Just thinking of all the other things I could be doing today."

"But instead you've chosen to spend time with your boyfriend's family," he murmured. "Well, aren't you the gracious one."

Ouch. She ignored the barely veiled jab. "Yes, I think I am actually." She tilted her head up at him in challenge. "Where are your parents, anyway? Or is this the part where you tell me they're not coming?"

"They're coming. Don't tell me you're afraid to be alone with me, Christy?"

No. Afraid of what I'd want to do to you if we were alone. "Sorry to break it to you, but we're in a major city at lunch time, during a work day. We're hardly alone."

"You didn't answer my question."

Christy shifted and tucked a strand of hair behind her ear. "I'm not afraid, Adam. Look, we've agreed to move forward, haven't we?"

"I guess we have. We certainly can't go backwards."

And he'd like that, she thought. If he could undo sleeping with her. The idea sent a pang of sadness through her. Well, *she* wouldn't regret it. No matter the mess now.

For the first two days Adam had been a great lover and friend, but as a foe she sensed he could make her life miserable. Who was she kidding—she was miserable.

From what Nate had told her, in business Adam could be ruthless. And when you brought a man's pride into the equation, things could get downright nasty.

"No, we can't go backwards," she murmured. What the hell. Being honest couldn't screw things up anymore than they already were. But it would feel good to say it. "And I wouldn't want to."

Something flared in Adam's eyes, and the cynical expression on his face seemed to waver.

"Hey, guys."

Christy glanced away from Adam to see Nate strolling down the street towards them. His parents were right behind him.

"Christy," Candace cried out as she hurried towards her with her hands outstretched. "You look lovely. So fashionable. Doesn't she look lovely, Nate? You've always appreciated good fashion on a woman."

"She looks great," Nate agreed dutifully.

"Don't you think she looks lovely, Adam?"

Christy winced and averted her gaze so she wouldn't have to see his reaction.

"Christy looks gorgeous," Adam murmured. "Almost edible."

"Edible?" Candace repeated with a confused look. "Sometimes I just don't understand you, Adam."

Thank God for that. Christy tried not to look too mortified. Edible? It was probably another reference to yesterday's breakfast moment. She closed her eyes. Oh God. Blueberries had forever lost their innocence.

Christy looked over at Nate just in time to see him roll his eyes.

"Now that we've established how lovely Christy is, do you think we could start the touring?" he asked dryly. "Christy suggested that we Ride the Duck."

Christy glared at him. Now why the hell had he brought that up? Being with Adam was hard enough. Sitting next to him on a duck on wheels would drive her positively insane.

"The Duck?" Adam repeated, looking at her. "Is that the weird-looking thing I keep seeing around town?"

"That's it. It does tours." Her smile turned tight. "It was actually a joke when I brought it—"

"Oh, it sounds wonderful!" Candace cooed. "Let's do it. Then I can tell everyone back home that I rode the Duck."

"All right, Mom, we'll do it," Adam answered and his smile grew as he stared at Christy and her unenthusiastic expression.

Nate's cell phone shrilled to life, and he excused himself.

"How far away is the Duck tour?" Steven asked. "Can we walk?"

Christy sighed. "No, we'll need to drive. It's up near the Space Needle."

Nate came back just then. Christy stared at him and knew the news wasn't going to be good.

"That was work. Apparently I had two employees call in sick during the day shift, and two of our phone carriers are down. Needless to say, we're slammed."

"So what does that mean, Nate?" Candace asked. "You don't have to go into work, do you?"

"Unfortunately, it looks like I do."

Thank God. She was off the hook. Christy almost yelped out loud at her stroke of good luck.

"Oh, what a shame," Adam said, clucking his tongue in disappointment. "But there's no reason Christy can't still spend the day with us, is there?"

Oh, he *didn't* just say that. Christy shot Adam a sharp glance. Seeing only feigned innocence there, she turned to Nate out of desperation.

"Err—I guess not," Nate agreed slowly. "If she wants to."

No! Of course I don't want to! She avoided everyone's gaze.

"Oh, please stay with us, Christy," Candace pleaded. "We'd love to spend the day with you and get to know you better. Unless you have somewhere else you'd rather be."

Uh, that'd be anywhere but here. But, Lord, she was weak when Candace started to beg. It was the whole sympathy for the mom thing.

"Oh, well..." She groaned inwardly. "I can't think of anything I'd rather do."

Adam stepped forward and laid a hand on her shoulder. Tingles moved through her entire body. "There you have it. Christy will stay with us while Nate heads off to work."

"Perfect." Nate grinned. "Then I'll see you later, honey."

Christy tried to silently convey her annoyance to Nate as he came up and drew her into his embrace. But apparently he was ignoring her efforts, and instead of just a hug, he planted a chaste kiss on her lips.

Ugh! She wanted to wipe her hand across the back of her mouth. God, it felt almost incestuous kissing Nate. He was like a brother to her. It also didn't help that she knew he was gay, and probably hated kissing her too.

Nate waved to them and then disappeared down the street again.

Christy turned back to Adam and his parents. Adam was

frowning, and the parents looked slightly confused.

"All right." She forced a smile. "Shall we go?"

"Sounds good to me. Well, since Adam and I both drive trucks," Steven began. "Why don't you take Christy up to the Duck, Adam, and your mom and I will meet you there?"

"Oh, I have my own car—"

"No need to waste gas," Adam interrupted. "Come ride with me. I won't bite."

Even if I want you to and that's the problem? For the second—or was it third—time that day, she found herself agreeing to something she didn't want to do. You're a pushover, Christy, she yelled silently. Then another voice acknowledged, *or maybe you just want to go with Adam anyway and you're using this as an excuse.*

As she climbed, literally, into Adam's humungous pickup, she cursed her bad luck.

"So, darlin', are you ready to have some fun?" Adam asked as he settled behind the wheel.

"Let the party start. I can hardly wait," she muttered sarcastically. Now that they were away from his parents, Christy saw no reason to stay in cheerful mode.

"Funny, the words sound positive, but your tone just doesn't ring true."

Christy sucked in her breath as his hand came to rest on her knee. She gave him a quick glance.

"What are you doing?"

"Just being friendly."

The tingles started up her leg. "Yes, but friendly between us tends to lead to a little more than friendly."

"And that's a problem because?"

His fingers were drawing circles on her leg and Christy felt her precious hold on staying immune slip away. *God, what was he doing?*

"It's a problem because..." Her mind went blank as his fingers dipped under her leg to trace the sensitive spot behind her knee. Even though her skirt acted as a barrier, it still had her trembling. "Because..."

"You have a boyfriend."

"*Right.* I have a boyfriend."

"My brother."

"Right. Nate." Ah, screw it. Christy closed her eyes and succumbed to the sensual caress.

Chapter Seven

Adam turned to look at her, running his gaze over her. Why couldn't he stop himself from touching her? Lord, how she tempted him.

That little kiss Nate had given Christy might have fooled his parents, but it wouldn't convince any person with a healthy sex drive. It had been almost comical. When they'd separated, he could have sworn Nate looked more than a little uncomfortable.

Maybe they were fighting and just putting on a happy face. But even that didn't seem right.

He continued to tease the soft area behind her knee, and didn't miss the way her breathing became heavier. He scowled. He needed to stop this. Take his hand away from her. But her skin was so soft and silky, and those little noises she made were so damn sexy.

Instead of questioning his brother's relationship with Christy, he should be questioning his own inability to leave her alone.

This was so out of character for him. But he couldn't seem to stop. He was like a smoker trying to quit, but always seemed to go back for another cigarette with the promise of *just one more time*. He'd been there already. Giving up smoking had been a breeze compared to giving up Christy. It was like he was addicted to her—and after just one night. And why the hell didn't she push him away?

"You know where it is, right?" she asked, her voice husky.

The spot to touch that makes you scream? Yeah, he knew. "Where what is?"

"Ride the Duck."

"I can figure it out." He knew where it was. He'd driven past it the two times he'd gone to her Salsa lessons.

The thought of her dancing in his arms, and moving her curvy body against him sent all the blood to his crotch.

He pulled his hand away from her leg and set it firmly back on the steering wheel. *Get some control, Adam.*

They arrived at the Duck tour a few minutes later and he was distracted by the need to find a parking spot. His parents were waiting for them when they finally went to buy their tickets.

"I've got everyone," Adam insisted when Christy went to pull out her wallet.

"That's not necessary."

"No, but since I'm the one who encouraged you to take some cheesy tour, the least I can do is pay for your trip."

"Point taken." Christy tucked her wallet back into her purse.

They got shuffled onto the nearly full Duck—which was really just a boat that could drive on land—and looked around for seating. His parents took two near the front that were open. Adam looked around, trying to find two more together.

"You're blocking the aisle." Christy grabbed his hand and tugged him towards the very back. "There's some back there."

He followed after her, his blood pounding faster at her touch. It was strange that she'd grabbed his hand...and it was strange that she'd let him touch her in the truck. Everything just seemed off kilter.

She shooed him into the seat first. "Since I live here, I don't really need a window seat."

"Thank you, darlin'." He forced an easy grin and slid past her. His arm brushed across the soft swell of her breast, and his smile became more strained. God, he wanted to hold that breast again, stroke her nipple until it was hard.

He made himself comfortable, unable to help noticing that she'd also been affected by the brief contact. Her nipples were rigid and distinctively outlined through her tank top. He bit back a groan. Why had he thought this was a good idea?

"So, tell me about Adam's Apples." Christy broke the silence, her voice somewhat unsteady.

He gave her a sidelong look, relieved for the distraction she was offering. "What do you want to know?"

"Well…I guess how it started and that kind of thing."

His eyebrows drew together. "Well, my parents raised Nate and me on a farm over in Eastern Washington. We had an apple orchard in the backyard—Mom would always bake apple pie on Sundays during the summer." He tried not to wince. Lord, that sounded like a sixties sitcom. "Apples have always kind of been a theme in my family."

The tour Duck started to move forward and he trailed off, glancing out the window.

"I went off to college to get a degree in business. While I was there, my friends and I thought it would be fun to brew our own beer."

"You brewed your own beer?" She giggled. "Were you just broke, or did you want to start up the next microbrewery?"

"We wanted to be the next microbrewery." He smiled. "But our beer turned out to be complete crap. When a bunch of frat boys won't even drink your beer, you know it's bad."

Christy's giggle turned into full-out laughter. "Where did you go to college?"

"Washington State."

"Me too," she cried in surprise. "When did you graduate?"

"Ten years ago. Which I'm sure makes me sound ancient to you."

"Right. And AARP called and said your card is in the mail." She rolled her eyes. "Please. I graduated three years ago. That's just crazy. Nate never told me you went to WAZZU."

At the mention of Nate, the intimate moment they were having seemed to waver and Adam withdrew a bit emotionally. *She's not yours, and never will be.*

She cleared her throat. "Anyway, how did you go from beer to apples?"

They were driving beside the waterfront now. Adam looked up in surprise as the people around them started making quacking noises at the driver's encouragement.

He shook his head. "So beer wasn't our strong point. But then one quarter I brought back some apples for the roomies. That's when I thought I'd try my hand at making hard cider."

"Ooo, I love hard cider. Did it work?"

"No, can't say that it did. That pretty much sucked, too. The others gave up at that point, but I kept trying things. I figured my luck with alcoholic beverages was nonexistent, and I oughtta target a PG audience."

"So you tried plain old apple cider?"

He dipped his head in acknowledgment. "I did. Now my product is simply apple cider."

"Ah, you see?" She nudged him. "You went from a college market to my high school students."

"I suppose I did."

"And it worked for you." The look she gave him clearly said she was in awe. "Everyone in Washington has heard of Adam's Apples."

She was really excited for him, proud of him. How great was that? Adam's pride went up another notch. So did his desire to have Christy for himself.

"It's already marketed regionally, I'm working on taking it national now."

"You're so ambitious. It shows." She winked. "Although I think your company name helps a little."

Adam laughed. He always got shit about that. "Too cheesy for you?"

"Mmm, actually it's pretty cute." She looked past him at Pioneer Square, where the tour was going through. "My apartment is a block that way."

"I remember." God, did he ever. Remembered their dinner together. Remembered licking her until she screamed on the kitchen table.

She looked sharply at him, having probably heard the husky timbre in his voice. Their gazes locked. She had to be thinking what he was thinking. About their night together.

Christy cleared her throat and then lowered her gaze.

"So, is it hard?" she asked. "Making apple cider?"

For a minute he'd thought she was asking if something else was hard. And his answer would have been an affirmative.

"Not too hard. I'll show you sometime."

And he probably would. *Lord. Just don't let it be with her as my sister-in-law.* The thought sent anger and a quiet desperation through him and tension coiled through his body. Maybe it was selfish of him, but he was really rooting for things not to work out between Christy and Nate.

"Are we going in the water?" he asked as the boat drove straight into Lake Union.

"Yup. I don't know if you caught it, but the driver was telling us how this vehicle was based on boats used during the Second World War."

"I must have missed it. Are you sure you've never been on this tour before?"

"Positive, it's just infamous around town."

"I gotcha." He settled back in his seat and looked out at the lake.

When the tour finally ended and they had to disembark, his parents were waiting for them.

His mom, smiling like it was Christmas, ran up to Christy and gave her a hug. "Oh, thank you, dear. I haven't had that much fun since...well since the barn dance at the Wilsons' farm last summer!"

"I'm glad you enjoyed it, Candace." Christy returned her hug and didn't seem the least bit uncomfortable by the intimacy.

Adam watched the two of them. Damn. It just didn't make sense. How could she be so friendly and innocent at times, and yet still be the kind of woman to cheat on her boyfriend?

"Will you be able to join us for dinner, Christy?" his father asked.

"Oh, I wish I could. But I teach a Salsa dancing class at seven," Christy apologized, shooting a quick glance at Adam. "Thank you so much for the invitation, though."

"All right. Well, Adam will drive you back to your car, dear. And we'll see you at dinner on Saturday. Thank you so much for the wonderful tour!"

His mom finally released her.

Christy smiled and waved goodbye to them. After his parents had driven off, Adam turned to face her.

"Do you have time for a cup of coffee?"

Christy looked up in surprise. He was asking her to coffee? Without the parents? Without Nate? Hmm. What she wouldn't give to know what he was thinking.

Finally, she just nodded. "I always have time for coffee. In fact, the shop where we first met is just a few blocks away if you want to walk there."

"I could use the exercise."

They set off, walking at an easy pace in silence. She brought up college again, and soon they were comparing notes on professors and classes they might have had in common.

When they reached Ooo La Latté, she went to open the door. Wait. Was that Nate? She glanced closer.

Damn, it *was*. He was supposed to be at work. *Bigger problem—he wasn't alone.* The other man with him leaned over to kiss Nate's cheek.

Christy spun around. "Actually there's a better place up the road."

Adam glanced in the door with a frown. "But—"

Before he could spot Nate and his boyfriend, Christy grabbed Adam's head and dragged his mouth down to hers.

First he went rigid against her, and then he groaned and drew her firm against him. She opened her mouth under his, her heart pounding when his tongue slipped inside.

The kiss had meant to be a distraction, but it suddenly took on a whole new light. It felt so good to have Adam like this again. Her mind spun with the smell of him, the taste of him.

With the essence of Adam.

He started to draw back and she came to her senses. *No!* No matter how mad she was at Nate right now, she couldn't let Adam see inside the shop.

She grabbed his hand and pulled him farther down the sidewalk. "I'm sorry. I probably shouldn't have done that, but it's been building up inside of me all day."

At least that wasn't a lie. She lifted her gaze to Adam's. He looked puzzled, and maybe even disturbed by the kiss. Great. Now he was probably going to freak out again.

"Look, I said I was sorry. I was out of line—"

He pushed her against the brick wall of a building and crushed his mouth down on hers, silencing her attempt to further justify the kiss.

Okay, so he wasn't mad. *God this was hot,* she decided as his tongue stroked over hers. He buried a hand in her hair, holding her head still and tilting his own to get better access to her mouth.

She groaned. She wanted this. All of this. It couldn't end here.

"Get a room."

The comment from a passerby made Adam jerk back from their almost frantic kiss.

Adam stared down at her, his thumb tracing over her mouth, which she knew must be swollen by now. She took a slow and steady breath, trying to clear her senses.

"Damn," he muttered.

And there it was. Staring into his eyes, Christy could see the exact moment when he regretted kissing her. It made her insides feel like they were shriveling up and rotting away.

A kiss like the one they'd just shared wasn't meant to be

lamented over. It was the type of kiss romance novels were written about. Or, hell, probably had a place in the porn industry. That kiss had been scorching.

"Don't say it." She raised a hand and lowered her gaze. "I know you're going to say it, but don't."

"Christy..."

"Oh, look, a cab." She stepped past him, waving down the taxi that was coming down the street.

The last thing she wanted to do was get into a discussion about how sleazy she was for cheating on her boyfriend—again. To see the accusation that would surely enter Adam's eyes.

Her stomach revolted just thinking about it.

"This isn't necessary. I'll drive you back to your car."

"Bye, Adam. I'll see you Saturday."

The taxi stopped next to her and she climbed inside before he could stop her.

Chapter Eight

"So, how was work?" Christy cradled the phone against her ear as she painted her toenails.

"Work? Oh! Yeah, it really blew. I'm so sorry I had to abandon you with the family, did you manage okay?"

Christy rolled her eyes. Right. Like the note of guilt in Nate's voice wasn't completely obvious.

"It was all right. The tour wasn't as bad as I thought." She stroked another layer of cotton candy pink over her big toenail. "And Adam was actually pretty decent to me."

"Really? See, he has his good moments. And at least you had fun."

How cute, he sounded so relieved. She'd give him another moment before going in for the kill.

"Yeah, actually we got along great. Actually, so great that Adam and I went for coffee afterwards."

"You did?" His voice rose sharply. "Where...did you go?"

She set down the polish and wiggled her toes to help them dry. "Oh, and did I forget to mention that I kissed him?"

"What? You what? Why! You're going to make him suspicious."

"Yeah, sorry about that," she went on blandly. "But it was either that, or let Adam watch you make out with your new boyfriend."

"I—oh." Pause. "Shit."

"Of course, maybe that wouldn't have been such a bad thing. He's going to find out sooner or later."

"Christy—"

"Hold on. First things first. Let me just clear this up." Christy smiled, almost enjoying his distress. Almost, but she was still a little too pissed. "You didn't get called into work today. You just thought it would be fun to ditch me with your family."

"No. That's not how it went." He sighed. Then finally, "I didn't lie about work calling. I did go in."

"Okay? So what happened?"

His voice shriveled. "I convinced the supervisor from the swing shift to come in early and pull a double."

Christy closed her eyes. Stay calm. She had to stay calm. "So instead of rejoining me and your family, you went off with your guy and left me to fend for myself?"

"I thought you'd be okay on your own. Everybody loves you. You're Christy."

"Not your brother! Your brother thinks I'm worse than cow shit right now. You didn't leave me to fend for myself, you threw me into a lion's den."

"He doesn't think you're cow shit—"

"Worse than cow shit," she interrupted. "Because now he thinks I've cheated on you, not just that night, but this afternoon, too."

"Well, maybe not. I mean, what kind of kiss are we talking about here?"

"*Nate.*"

"Okay, okay. I'm sorry, Christy. It was a shitty thing for me to do."

"Damn straight."

There was a long pause.

"So...you saw me and Brian?"

"Yup."

"Okay, tell me. Didn't you think he was cute?"

"What?" He couldn't be serious. He could not be serious. "We're not discussing the cuteness of your new boyfriend. We're discussing your screwed up way of thinking."

"Okay, okay, I shouldn't have—"

"I can't deal with you right now." Christy slammed her phone shut.

Most of the time Nate was a loyal friend whom she loved dearly. Then there were the times he had his head up his ass. Lately he seemed to be taking residency up there.

She walked to kitchen, her toes curled upward so the polish wouldn't smudge.

God. And she still had to teach class in a half-hour. Which meant no dinner for her.

Christy peeled a banana. This would just have to do.

He was here. Christy's breath hitched and she hesitated to walk through the door of the dance studio. Adam was leaning against the wall, watching her—waiting for her.

She shouldn't have kissed him today. What was he doing here? Why had he come? She lifted her chin and strode over to him.

"Did you come tonight for a refund?"

"A refund?" His lips twisted into a mocking smile. "No,

darlin', I came to get my money's worth."

She blinked. "You're staying for the class?"

"Is that a problem?"

Christy hesitated before shaking her head. "No. It's not a problem. You signed up for it. I just assumed that since you didn't show last night..."

Adam gave her a brief smile. "I know what you assumed."

Bullshit. He didn't know the first thing about what she had assumed. She had assumed that he'd only taken the classes to sleep with her. Once he'd succeeded there was no reason to come back. So what the hell was he doing here?

Oh no. She glanced away from him uneasily. Was Adam one of those men who always wanted what they couldn't have? Had she just become a challenge? Someone who was no longer attainable, therefore more desirable?

Stop it. She shook her head to clear that train of thought. It was ridiculous to even be analyzing this. She just had to keep things professional.

"Well then, welcome back, Adam. Please find yourself a partner because we'll be starting soon."

He stopped her from leaving by circling his fingers around her wrist. She gave a small tug to try to break free, and then narrowed her gaze when he refused to let her go.

"I have a class to teach, Adam. Do you mind giving me my arm back?"

"You're my partner."

So he did want her. "Oh, I'm sorry," she said, enjoying the way his eyes darkened. "Since you weren't here last night, I've chosen someone new to dance with."

"He can find someone else."

Christy's eyes widened in disbelief. Talk about caveman

mentality. "I'm sorry, Adam, but you'll have to find a new partner. I'm not dancing with you tonight."

She jerked her wrist free and went to find Carlos. He was surrounded by a group of simpering women who were discussing the Salsa club scene in Seattle.

"Can I talk to you?" she said after the group began to disperse.

"Sure, niña. Que pasa?"

"Can you dance with me tonight? I know it's not the norm, but Adam is here and we've had a falling out of sorts."

"So you'd rather not dance with him?" He gave her a wide smile. "You Americans spend so much time fighting rather than loving. I think you should dance with him. He is good for you, niña."

"*Carlos, please.* Now's not the time to play matchmaker." Christy groaned. "I told him I had a new partner, but the guy I danced with last night isn't here."

"Christy, you know I would," he said finally. "But old Ruthie is my partner. I'm sorry, niña, but you're going to have to dance with el Diablo. At least until we start rotating partners."

Christy cursed under her breath and then walked back to where Adam stood watching her. Damn him. He was enjoying this.

"I take it we're still partners?"

"Yeah, don't you feel lucky?" she grumbled and took his hand, leading him to the middle of the floor.

"With you in my arms? Very."

Jeez, she thought in amazement, it was like he didn't care anymore that she was supposedly with Nate. Like he'd just said, screw it, I want her, she's mine.

Wouldn't that be nice?

The music started. She moved to step forward on the second beat, but he pushed her back and took the lead.

"You know, I think I've gotten the hang of this Salsa thing," he said conversationally. "So you won't mind if I lead from now on?"

"Go for it. Just don't screw up." Okay, that might have been a little bitchy. She winced and glanced away from him.

Adam just laughed, seeming satisfied that she didn't try to resist him taking over the lead.

She continued to dance with him. Surprisingly enough, he was doing pretty well. Still, it was a relief when the time came to rotate partners. But all too soon that came to an end and she again found herself in his arms.

He pressed his hips close to hers. She closed her eyes, trying not to think about the part of him that pressed blatantly against her. Trying not to acknowledge the heavy pressure that built between her legs.

"Enjoying yourself, darlin'?" he murmured. "I have to say, you've always impressed me with how well you move."

Her heart thudded at the innuendo. "Why did you show up tonight, Adam? Really."

"What's wrong with a guy wanting to learn how to dance?"

"If that were the case, you wouldn't have insisted on dancing with me. Anyone should have done."

"But you're the teacher. And I've always had a thing for teachers."

"I feel sorry for your teachers," she muttered, shaking her head, smiling despite herself. "I'll bet you were a favorite in the principal's office."

"Now how'd you know that?" he drawled.

"Lucky guess."

"Want to get a beer with me after this?"

What was he up to now? "I thought cider was your thing now?"

"Every man likes a good beer now and then. So what do you say?"

She should say no. It wouldn't help things. Just put them both into temptation's path again.

"It can be innocent, Christy."

"Yeah, as innocent as your hard-on right now?"

He gave her a casual shrug. "Hell, I can't help Junior. He's got a mind of his own."

Christy laughed, relaxing a little. "Innocent, huh?"

"Sure."

"Well—" she glanced down at his hand on her waist, "—I can't say no to beer, especially since you're buying."

"Now that's what I like to hear, darlin'. A woman who likes her beer."

"Yeah, you and every other man."

He laughed and her stomach filled with warmth. She enjoyed his laugh, hell, she just enjoyed him. Whether they were having a serious conversation, or bantering back and forth like a wild game of tennis. He was charming and he was funny. There just wasn't a whole lot that she didn't like about Adam.

Except for their whole situation of course.

"I think we're supposed to stop now."

Adam's comment had her snapping out of auto-mode. The music had ended and Carlos was dismissing the class. *Welcome back to earth, Christy.*

Poor Carlos. She'd pretty much shirked all teaching

responsibility tonight. Then again, she'd warned Carlos that she was out of her comfort zone. He knew when to take over.

She sighed and followed Adam outside.

"Is my truck okay?" he asked, leading her over to where it was parked under the street lamp.

"Sure. As long as I get to pick where we go." Christy waited for him to unlock her door and then climbed up into the passenger seat. Her hands trembled just the tiniest bit. *Was this a bad idea?*

"So where are you taking me?" he asked, once seated behind the wheel. He started the engine and gave her a sideways look.

"Turn left here, and then left on Mercer."

A few minutes later they were parked outside a bar with the rampant sounds of karaoke pouring out the door.

"You like this type of scene?" he asked with a dubious expression as they walked inside.

"Every once in a while."

Her real reason for bringing him here was because it was safe. No dark corners or intimate atmosphere. Just loud, drunken twenty-somethings attempting to sing the latest rap song. The stale smell of beer permeated the air.

"Is this place owned by a fraternity?" Adam drawled as his gaze drifted around the bar.

"I admit the crowd is a little young." She walked up to the bar and managed to catch a free bartender. "One Mac and Jack. What'll you have, Adam?"

"Budweiser."

Christy rolled her eyes. He was a total cowboy through and through.

"I'll try to find us a table." She left him to pay for the drinks and threaded her way through the crowd.

She managed to find a table, though it was littered with empty plates and beer glasses. She pushed them towards the wall, and slid into the booth. The table itself was covered in stains. The seats of the booth were made of a rubbery plastic that was splitting, emitting foam every few inches.

When Adam came back with the beers a few minutes later, she forced a smile.

"One beer for the city girl," he declared and set it down across from her. "And one beer for me."

"The cowboy."

"Yeehaw." He shifted abruptly. "I think the booth just bit me."

"No, you probably just got caught in one of the cracks. The seats are kind of falling apart."

"Ah, I see." He gave her that slow grin that always made her pulse kick up a notch. "This is a real nice place. Thanks for bringing me, Christy."

"Fine, I admit it. It's kind of a dump, but it's got personality. And it used to be even worse before the whole anti-smoking law came into effect."

"Personality. Sure. So where's the bull?"

"The bull?"

"Yeah, the mechanical bull."

Christy laughed as she shook her head at him. "There's only one bar in this city that I know has a bull. And that's only because they have a country theme."

"Now that's a damn shame."

Someone started singing another karaoke song, and Adam shot a lethal glance in his direction.

"That man deserves a good ass-kicking for trying to sing Toby Keith."

Christy squinted at him. "Who's Toby Keith?"

He groaned. "See, this is why we wouldn't have worked out. You don't even like country music."

She barely heard the last part of his sentence, she was still focused on the *this is why we wouldn't have worked out* part. Had he considered them *working* for a while? Had it been more than a one-night stand for him?

"Christy?"

"What?"

"You got all dazed looking for a minute there. Are you okay?"

"I'm fine," she said absently. "I was just listening to the guy sing for a minute. You're right, he's terrible." She reached for her beer, drinking a quarter of it in one swallow.

"Wow."

She set the pint back down and looked back at him. "Tell me something."

"Anything, darlin'."

"That darlin' thing is getting a little distracting." She shook her head. "Anyway. When you had sex with me...were you planning on calling me after you left the next morning?"

He leaned back in the booth and whistled. "That was out of left field."

"Was it?" Christy challenged, deciding being straightforward was her best approach. "There's no need to keep playing games, Adam. Let's just be honest with each other."

"All right, why don't you tell me what's really going on between you and Nate?"

Okay, maybe straightforward hadn't been the best idea. He didn't miss a thing.

"Nate and I..." she hesitated. What kind of lie did she tell now?

There had to be a way she could answer all questions truthfully and not give up Nate's cover. She was so tired of trying to be the good girlfriend in a relationship that didn't exist.

"I don't think we're going to stay together much longer."

Adam stared at her, replaying in his head what she'd just told him. *Don't get your hopes up, buddy.* And how would Nate feel if he knew his girlfriend was talking bad about their relationship? For once though, he wasn't convinced that what she'd told him was a lie.

"All right I told you mine," she interrupted his thoughts. "Now tell me yours."

"Mine?"

"Would you have called?"

Adam winced. Not because the answer was bad, but because he'd been guilty of not calling other women in the past. But with Christy he'd known that very night that with her it would be different. He'd had to force himself not to call her an hour after leaving her apartment.

"I would have called." He picked up his beer. "The situation just ended up being a little—"

"Messed up," she muttered.

He saw the quick look of disgust and anger that passed over her features. There it was again, the sensation that something wasn't right with everything. And what was she thinking, because she looked awfully frustrated.

Christy looked up at him and her expression changed. As if she'd realized she'd done something wrong.

There was just something he couldn't put his finger on.

"How's your beer?" Her voice sounded strained.

"Same every time I have one. Good."

"Good." Her hands looked tiny wrapped around her own pint. "So you go back to Eastern Washington on Sunday?"

"That's the plan."

No he hadn't imagined it. She'd looked disappointed for a minute. Maybe she was just upset that her man-on-the-side would be taken out of the equation.

She glanced into her beer. "Are you coming to class tomorrow?"

"We'll see how things go." He wasn't sure he could handle being that close to her again. He was already at the threshold of temptation. "Are you still coming to dinner on Saturday?"

Her smile was faint. "Yeah, I'll be there. I like your parents quite a bit. They're sweet."

"They're good people. Tell me something, why did you decide to become a Spanish teacher?"

Christy looked surprised and relieved at the subject change.

"Easy enough," she answered with a smile. "I was good at Spanish in high school, and even spent a year in Spain as an exchange student. I figured that since I love the language so much, I should teach it. Not to mention the whole summers off thing."

Adam joined in her soft laughter. "But you're still working as a dance instructor."

"Actually, just this week," she admitted. "Carlos usually teaches and I help out every now and then, but he gave me the reins for this week. I just wanted to give it a go and see what I thought. I like it, but I think I need my summer for downtime."

"So you're not teaching next week?" he asked, an idea forming in his head. An idea of maybe taking the city girl out of the city. He knew it wasn't the smartest one, but he wasn't ready to discard it just yet.

"Nope. Next week I plan to sit on my butt and do nothing."

Adam finished off his beer and looked to see how much she had left. Apparently she'd passed him by a few minutes ago.

"You were thirsty."

"Ya think? Dancing for an hour straight does that to you."

"Do you want to get out of here?" Adam asked, reaching out to touch her hand. He heard the sharp breath she drew in, and his own pulse jacked up a notch.

"Yes."

Her gaze met his. Her pupils were dilated, her breathing was uneven. She still wanted him. The signs were all there. She broke the contact, averting her gaze and sliding out of the booth.

Adam gritted his teeth, staring at the sexy curve of her ass. That temptation threshold was crumbling, slowly, but surely. He stood up and followed her out of the bar.

They stepped outside and the noise dropped to a muted roar. Thank God. Not even for Christy would he go back to that place. If she ever came over the mountains, he'd show her what a real bar was like.

His earlier idea once again flickered through his head. It was gaining momentum.

"Are you cold?" Adam asked as he unlocked the passenger door to his truck. Christy had her arms folded in front of her chest, and he saw a shiver pass through her.

"A bit. Nothing a little car heat won't cure," she answered and climbed into the truck.

Adam went around to his door, already shrugging out of his flannel shirt. He had a T-shirt underneath and was still hot from being squashed into that hellhole.

"Here, put this on."

Christy caught the flannel with a look of surprise. "You didn't need to take off your shirt."

"My mama raised me right, darlin'." He deliberately inflected an accent as he shut the door to the truck.

She laughed as she slipped her arms into the shirt, leaving it unbuttoned. It was so big that it almost went to her knees. She looked ridiculous. And sexy as hell.

"See, you could easily be a local," she told him. "You've got the flannel shirt and everything."

"I thought the grunge movement died out."

"It did, but I'm not sure all of Seattle got the memo."

Adam's grin widened. "I like your humor, Christy."

"What else do you like?" she quipped with an impish grin. Her cheeks reddened and she dropped her gaze. "Oh God. Sorry, sometimes it just pops out before I think about it."

Lord it was hard to resist her. Especially when she was flirting so adorably. Which should've been a problem in itself, Adam reminded himself. She didn't have the right to flirt.

"I don't mind." Why *didn't* he mind? And why wasn't he starting the truck and driving away from this intimate moment?

"You don't?" She looked so damn surprised and hopeful.

"Darlin', sometimes I want you the way I had you on Tuesday." Sometimes? Hell, all the time. But he was better than that. He was, damn it. He wouldn't seduce his brother's girlfriend. Again. "But it just can't happen."

"Says who?" Christy's tongue did that sexy swipe over her lips, her eyes bright and intense.

"Rules." Adam clenched his fists, the only way he could stop himself from touching her. *Get a hold of yourself, buddy.*

"You know what they say about rules. They're made to be broken." She slid across the seat towards him. Her warm body pressed close to his. "I need you to do something for me, Adam."

"What's that?" Tresses of her hair tickled his chin and he could smell the flowery scent of her shampoo.

She raised her head and locked her gaze with his. "I need you to trust me when I say that nothing is as it seems."

That wasn't exactly what he'd expected her to say.

"What isn't what it seems, Christy?"

She hesitated and then sighed, shaking her head. "That's all I can say."

Lord she was making this hard on him.

"Do you trust me, Adam?"

He wanted to. Her intensity seemed so sincere, her desperation for him to say yes, puzzling. And God, he wanted her so bad.

"Your silence speaks for itself." She started to slide away. "I don't have the right to ask you to trust me anyway."

The loss of her warmth pressed against him spurred Adam into action. He turned, wrapping his hands around her waist. She seemed surprised, but didn't protest, as he settled her on his lap. She shifted, leaning back against the door.

"I trust you, Christy." He rubbed his thumb over her mouth, which parted on a sigh. "I think I'm probably crazy to do so, but for some reason I trust you."

Her frustration was evident. "Adam—"

"Shh." He increased the pressure with his thumb, until he felt the moist softness of her mouth around the tip.

She leaned forward, her hair falling in a curtain, trapping them in a different world and upping the intimacy of the moment. Adam slid his hands up to cup her face, bringing her mouth down to his.

She was so soft. Her mouth, her body. The curve of her breast pressed against his arm through his flannel she wore. He moved his hands up and down her back, stroking her delicate body as his tongue rubbed against hers.

Her hands moved to the zipper on his jeans, and he grabbed her wrist to stop what she was trying to do.

"Not a good idea, darlin'."

"Actually, a very good idea, cowboy." Her soft breath tickled his mouth as she laughed. "Please let me, it's all I've thought about since the other night."

"Someone might see us." His excuses were weak. He knew it. She knew it. And she'd succeeded in unbuttoning his jeans and getting his zipper down.

"You parked away from the street lamps, and everyone's inside. No one will see us."

She freed him from his boxers and his cock stood rigid out of his jeans, contradicting his protests.

"Just trust me, Adam," she murmured, sliding her hand down to touch him.

Chapter Nine

All thoughts left his brain and went south as her tongue traced over his neck. Then she bit him just a little harder than gently.

"Would you like my mouth to be down there?" Her hands squeezed his dick lightly.

God yes. Yes! When he didn't answer aloud, she gave a soft laugh and slithered down his chest so that her head was in his lap. A moment later her tongue curled around the head of his erection and he groaned—the sound loud and guttural in the car. She responded by taking him into her mouth, slowly, inch by inch.

"Sweet Jesus, darlin'." He gasped, arching his hips to send his cock deeper into her warm, wet mouth.

Christy's hands dipped down to cup his sac, while her mouth moved up and down on him, mimicking what she'd done earlier with her hand.

Adam stared down at her, his breathing hard and labored. As she made love to him with her mouth, he reached down to delve a hand into her tank top and cup one of her breasts.

His fingers found her hard nipple. It aroused him further to know that she was turned on by what she was doing to him. He pinched it lightly between his thumb and forefinger, pulling it out to its full length. His other hand dipped into the back of her skirt and caressed one round cheek of her ass.

Christy moaned in response—her mouth and hand worked harder to bring him pleasure.

"Christy," he gasped. "I'm going to come if you don't stop soon, darlin'."

She pulled her mouth from him and glanced at him through her lashes.

"I don't suppose you have a condom now, do you?"

He reached past her and popped open the glove compartment. "Actually, a whole darn box."

She grabbed the box and ripped it open, pulling a condom free and opening it just as quickly.

"Are you sure about this?" he asked. "We can drive—"

"I can't wait." She rolled the condom onto him and then moved to straddle him.

"Good. I was hoping you'd say that." He pushed her skirt to her waist and tugged her soaked thong to the side.

His cock nudged between her thighs, seeking the soft wet heat of her center.

"Hurry," she begged and lowered herself just slightly onto him.

Grasping her hips, he plunged upward into her core.

"Oh!" Her arms wrapped around his shoulders and she buried her face in the curve of his neck.

"Ride me," he whispered hoarsely, pressing his hips forward to bury himself deeper inside her. "Move on me, darlin'."

She drew in a ragged breath and lifted her head from his neck. Closing her eyes, she bit her lip and started a slow undulation on his cock.

His eyes crossed and his breathing grew harsh. She moved faster, seeming to find her own rhythm.

Adam's glance drifted out the car window, half convinced there'd be an audience watching them. But even if there was, he wouldn't have seen them on the darkened street.

He slipped his hands underneath her tank top to cover her breasts. The nipples were tight and poked against his palms.

"So sweet," he whispered, pinching the tips.

She groaned and moved harder on him, her nails digging into his shoulders now.

"I'm going to come," she whispered. "I'm so close…"

Wanting to push her over the edge, he slipped one hand back down her stomach and between her legs.

One touch of his finger against her swollen clit and her muscles convulsed around him, her body arching into his.

He watched her eyes slam shut and her mouth form into a perfect "O" as she climaxed.

The image alone pushed him near the edge. Sent a wave of something primal through him and his balls tightened.

"*Adam.*" Her husky whisper was the final straw.

He choked out a gasp and closed his eyes, emptying himself again and again until he lay weak against the seat.

His head dropped back against the headrest and he looked at the ceiling of the truck. "That was incredible."

"Oh God, yes." She drew in an unsteady breath and climbed off him.

Adam fumbled to remove the condom and placed it in his makeshift plastic trash bag in the back seat.

"Come back to my condo," he said, before really thinking about it.

"Your condo?" she repeated with surprise. "I thought you were in a hotel."

"I own a condo downtown. It makes it convenient since I do a lot of business here." He touched her cheek. "We could do what we just did again...several times. Then I'll take you home first thing in the morning."

"Oh." She turned to look out the window. "I...I'd better not."

Damn. What was she thinking now? He'd seen the shutters go down. Something he'd said had put her guard up. Adam laid a hand on her shoulder, and turned her to look at him.

"Are you okay, Christy? I wouldn't feel right knowing I made you do something that you didn't want to."

"No, of course you didn't," she said hurriedly as her cheeks reddened. "I wanted to do...what we did. I enjoyed it and I hope you did as well."

"There's no doubt about it, darlin'." He smiled and played with a wayward strand of her hair. "Thank you."

"Thank you." She gave a small smile before lowering her gaze. "I'd better get home. Do you mind just dropping me at my car?"

Shit. Something was wrong. Adam started the engine and pulled his truck out of the shadow of its parking spot. They didn't speak during the few minutes it took to get back to her car. And when he pulled up next to her Beetle, her hand was already on the door handle.

"Christy?"

"Yes?" She looked at him almost reluctantly.

He didn't even know what he planned on saying, but it probably wouldn't have been appropriate. Hell, everything in the last two days hadn't been appropriate.

So he just squeezed her hand and said, "I'll see you later."

"Okay." She was out of the truck before the word was even out of her mouth. She slammed the door and ran to her car.

Adam waited for her to get inside and start the engine before he backed out of the parking lot.

༺༻

This was getting to be a bad habit, Christy decided as she sat on the couch, scooping up Rocky Road. She couldn't keep turning to chick flicks and ice cream whenever she had man problems.

And the situation with Adam was definitely a problem. Every time she thought about what they'd done in his truck, she got all flustered and aroused. Not to mention feeling a little slutty.

God, what Adam must think of her now. He still figured she was Nate's girlfriend. And the way he'd invited her back to his condo for the night, with the promise of getting her home early...he'd probably written her off as being slutty and easy. Well, with him she was easy. Completely.

Not to mention she did screw his brains out in his truck on a public street. Christy stabbed her spoon deeper into the ice cream and scowled. *Argh! This was just so frustrating.*

Maybe Adam was taking her seriously when she'd told him she and Nate were on the verge of breaking up. And technically, since it was Saturday, they were. Tomorrow she would be a free woman again. Her bargain with Nate would be fulfilled. Would Adam still want her though?

She was beginning to wonder. He hadn't showed up to the final class last night—which added to her humiliation. Maybe he'd lost all respect for her after that spicy episode in his truck, presuming he'd had any to begin with.

Her cell rang and she grabbed it off the couch. *Let it be Adam!* She scowled when Nate's name popped up—she still wasn't ready to talk to him after the stunt he'd pulled the other day. He'd pretty much ensured himself the top spot on her shit list.

Hmm. But maybe he was calling regarding dinner tonight. She answered her phone.

"Come on, you've got to forgive me, Christy!" he wailed the moment she said hello.

"Oh, relax. I'm coming tonight."

"Fantastic. Are you still sleeping with Adam?"

"Nate!"

"Just curious," he said defensively. "I'm not judging you. I was just wondering if my always honorable brother would be the type to steal his brother's girlfriend."

Christy ground her teeth together and, for the first time in their friendship, refused to share the facts of her sex life.

"What time is dinner?"

"Seven at Palisades. I'll pick you up."

"I think I'd rather drive myself."

"It wouldn't look right," Nate protested. "We need to show up together."

"But we're breaking up tomorrow, so why not give them something to wonder about now?" Christy pointed out. "That way it's not a complete surprise when you tell them we've split."

"You really won't drive with me?"

"I'm going to have to say no on this one, Nate. I'll see you there."

She shut her phone and felt a sense of pride fill her. It

might have been regarding a petty matter, but she'd finally said no to Nate. She was such a doormat sometimes.

Christy picked up her ice cream again and turned her attention back to the movie on the television. Watching the character in the movie get a makeover gave her an idea.

She grabbed her phone again and dialed number five on her speed dial.

"Hey, Heather, how busy are you?" she asked when her cousin picked up the phone.

"Not really. I have a one o'clock appointment, then nothing until four," Heather snorted. "It's dead as hell here today. Why, what's up?"

"Hmm. Think you could fit me in for a trim and then maybe do something fun with my hair?"

"Sure, get your ass in here. I haven't seen you in weeks."

"Great." Christy glanced at the clock. "Give me a half-hour and I'll be right down."

She shut the phone and ran to grab a quick shower.

The bell over the door signaled her arrival at her cousin's small salon.

Heather, who'd been in the midst of sweeping up hair on the floor, looked up and grinned.

"Hey, Cuz. Glad you could make it in."

Christy crossed the room and threw her arms around her cousin for a hard hug.

"Ah, what's going on? The last time you clutched me this tight, you'd just been told you needed another tetanus shot."

Christy drew in an unsteady breath and released Heather,

smiling sheepishly.

"Sorry," she muttered and thrust a hand through her hair. "I think I just needed a hug from someone who doesn't think I'm a complete whore, or isn't milking me dry with asinine favors."

Heather's mouth gaped and she tilted her head. "Well. I take it we have a lot to catch up on."

"It's not that complex. I just agreed to pretend to be the girlfriend of my gay best friend. Not knowing that I'd just screwed his older brother—whom I'd never met before a few days ago." She sniffled. "Now Adam probably thinks I'm the sluttiest of sluts since I can't keep my hands off him when I supposedly have a boyfriend—Nate."

Heather blinked. "Well, shit. That makes perfect sense. Or it would if I were on crack." She gestured to the chair. "Come sit down and start from the beginning while I trim your split ends."

Christy sidled over to the hair station and sat down, then proceeded to tell all about the past few days.

When she was done, Heather had trimmed off an inch of hair and was giving her a curious look in the mirror.

"You're really falling for this guy."

"Am I? Oh, I wouldn't say—"

"No, it wasn't a question. I was stating a fact." Heather lifted a finger at her in the mirror. "You need to stop this bullshit with Nate and then pursue this thing with Adam."

"Yeah, that's kind of my plan."

"Today. At dinner. You walk in there looking like you mean business, and then you walk out later knowing you and Adam have a chance. Because this guy sounds too fucking good to let go." Heather grinned. "Now you've got to let me try something with your hair."

"I'm in your hands," Christy murmured, already feeling better about things.

She watched her cousin scurry about, grabbing a brush and some hair clips. How often had she envied her older cousin while growing up? So fun and free-spirited, not to mention gorgeous. Blonde, curvy, she was like some pin-up queen from years past. Though she did have a bit of a potty mouth.

"So, what about you, Cuz, dating anyone?"

Heather glanced up and shrugged. "Somewhat. I've been seeing this one guy, Barry. He's okay, but not so great in bed."

"And we know how important that is." Christy giggled.

"Definitely. Anyway, I'm supposed to go with him tomorrow to some big family barbeque. I can't say I'm looking forward to it—his family is kind of wealthy and...yuppie to the extreme."

"Gotcha. Keep me posted."

"I will."

"But Christy, promise me you'll stop this crap with Nate." Heather squeezed her shoulder and met her gaze in the mirror. "You've had worse luck with men than me. And you deserve to be happy."

Christy gave a slow nod as her cousin went back to fiddling with her hair. Heather was right. She really did deserve it. The question was, did she have the nerve to tell Nate the deal was off?

After leaving her cousin's salon a half-hour later, Christy swung by Ooo La Latté to grab a cappuccino.

Her nerves were shot with the prospect of this last dinner with Nate and his family, and caffeine would help de-stress her.

"Hey there, Christy. Do you want your usual?" Madison grinned from behind the counter.

"Hi, Madison. Thanks, the usual is great."

"All right. Love the hair, by the way."

"Thanks."

Madison rang up her drink order. "So, I haven't seen you in a few days."

"Yeah, I've been a little distracted..." she murmured vaguely and handed over her money. "How are things going?"

"Things are amazing. Absolutely amazing. Okay, I have to share." Madison grinned and then thrust her left hand over the counter with a squeal. "Gabe and I got engaged!"

"Oh, Madison..." Christy sighed and took the other woman's hand, admiring the moderate ring on her finger. "How wonderful for you both. I'm so happy for you guys."

And she was. Though, it did give her that familiar ache. To know someone else had found and settled down with the love of her life...and meanwhile she was stuck in some ridiculous charade, possibly losing her only chance at love. But no. Not anymore, she vowed.

"So how have you been?" Madison's gaze softened, her gaze sincere. "Anyone special in the picture?"

She shrugged and forced a smile. "Possibly. We'll have to see."

There was a time when things hadn't been so easygoing between her and Madison. When their mutual friend had tried to set Christy up with Gabe, before realizing Gabe and Madison were dating. But that crunchy time had passed, and they had both moved on without any hard feelings.

"Well, you'll meet someone." Madison winked and handed her the cappuccino the barista had prepared. "I have no doubt about it."

"Thanks, Madison. I'll see you later." Christy waved and

walked back out to her car.

Once inside, she shut the door and stared at the coffee shop. So Madison would be the next girl in line to get her happily ever after. *Heather's right. I deserve to be happy. I deserve my own happily ever after, too.*

And she'd get it, she decided, and jumped back in the car. Tonight, things were going to change.

Adam lifted his wine glass and took a sip, glancing again at the empty spot at the table. Nate looked nervous. He must be panicking that Christy hadn't showed up yet.

He hoped she wouldn't stand them all up. It would throw a wrench in his plans. Adam looked again at his brother.

Nate was blotting his face with a napkin and shooting desperate looks towards the lobby of the restaurant every few minutes.

"She'll be here any minute. She said she might be running a bit late."

"Should we order?" Adam asked, raising an eyebrow.

Maybe Nate and Christy really were about to end things. Or maybe Christy's absence had something to do with what had happened between them two nights ago. Her abrupt change in attitude still bothered him. Did she regret it? He sure didn't. He would hold that memory with him until he was too old to get an erection.

"No, let's wait for Christy," his mom protested. "I do love that girl, she's so sweet."

Adam hid a smile. He could vouch for that. She was sweet indeed. And not just from that bubbly personality. Every square inch of her body was sweet and kissable.

He closed his eyes and remembered the taste and smell of her, especially the musky sweetness between her legs that he could entice.

He opened his eyes and his gaze connected with Nate's. Nate was staring at him with a contemplative look. Guilt stabbed low in his gut, but it didn't overshadow the feelings he had for Christy. He couldn't regret what had happened between them. But, God what a mess.

"Oh, no, have you guys been here long?"

Everyone turned to look as Christy came hurrying over to their table.

"I could have sworn you said seven-thirty, Nate." Christy sat down, not beside Nate, but in the chair beside Adam.

Nate's eyes widened, but a smile somehow appeared on his face and he gave a stiff shrug.

"I clearly said seven, but let's not worry about that right now, okay?"

"Okay." Christy laughed and smiled up at Adam.

He glanced down at her upturned face and wondered what she was up to. She looked all business and sexy as hell in a black suit. He had the urge to pull the chopsticks—or whatever they were—out of her hair and release her tendrils from the severe knot on her head.

"Oh. You didn't order?" she asked, glancing around in surprise. A look of guilt crossed her smooth features. "I'm sorry. You should have gone ahead without me."

Hmm. Adam's gaze narrowed and he wondered briefly if she'd planned to be late. But then that wouldn't make any sense.

"Of course not, dear. We haven't been here too long." Adam's father smiled gently at her. "Would you like a glass of wine when the waiter comes back?"

"That would be lovely. I'll have the house Chardonnay. I'm not too picky." She glanced down at Adam's glass and he wondered if she had known that's what he was drinking.

If anyone speculated why Christy had chosen to sit next to Adam instead of Nate, they didn't comment on it. Instead the conversation stayed light and comfortable until after they ordered and were waiting for their food.

His parents had chosen the salmon, while he and Christy had ordered steaks. Only Nate ordered a vegetarian dish that made Adam cringe when he saw it.

Halfway through dinner, he decided it was time to make the announcement.

Adam cleared his throat and set down his fork. "I was talking with Mom and Dad. And we all thought it would be nice if you both could come over to see us next week."

There was a moment of stunned silence at the table. Nate looked surprised and more than a little horrified.

Christy glanced up at Adam and he saw the flicker of excitement in her eyes. She liked the idea. But then she glanced at Nate and he could sense when her excitement turned to frustration.

"We'd have to talk about it," she replied slowly.

"I have to work," Nate protested with a shake of his head.

"All week? You don't have any days off?" their dad asked.

"I have the weekend off."

"Why doesn't Christy come over and spend the week with us, and you can join us on the weekend?" their mom suggested. "The poor girl needs a vacation, don't you, sweetie?"

"I haven't had one in a while," she agreed right away. "And I've heard so much about your home that I feel like I should see it now."

"Then you should come." Adam nodded his head as he took another bite of his baked potato. "We'd love to have you."

"We'll have to talk about it." Nate echoed her earlier words. "And let you know in the morning."

Christy's gaze dropped back to her plate as she prodded a baby carrot with her fork.

When dinner was finally over, Adam reached for the bill. His parents tried to fight for it, but he wouldn't have it. Once again, Nate made no move to argue or offer to help pay. Christy tried to hand him her share, but he waved her money aside.

"I do hope you decide to come," his mother told Christy, giving her another hug. "You'd love Peppertown."

"I've driven through, but never really stopped to visit." Christy lowered her voice. "I'll see if I can't convince Nate."

"Wonderful!"

"Have a good drive back," Christy said, pausing to give his dad a hug too.

When she'd finished with his parents, she turned to face Adam and gave him a searching look.

"Maybe I'll see you next week," she said softly.

"We hope you can make it." He knew that their voices carried, so he kept the conversation neutral. "Thank you for everything you've done for us this week. I can honestly say that I had an amazing trip."

She smiled, her gaze searching his. "I did too."

He took her hand and gave it a quick squeeze. "I'll be seeing you."

"Have a good drive home."

"Will do." He dropped her hand and turned to walk away.

God, she just had to come over the mountains to stay with them. He needed that extra week to feel out what was going on between them. To try to understand the complexities of Christy and Nate's relationship—if there even was one still.

Dinner had been interesting, to say the least. His parents were probably in their car discussing the Christy and Nate situation at this very moment.

When he climbed into his truck a few minutes later, he glanced back at the restaurant in time to see Christy and Nate emerge. They were arguing something fierce. But Nate looked a little more upset than Christy, who shrugged and finally walked away from him.

Very interesting indeed. He pulled out of the parking lot and headed for the freeway to start his long drive home. *Come on, Christy, tell him you want to go.*

Christy climbed into her car, giving Nate a stoic glance when he came running up to the door.

"I'm sorry I yelled at you." He sighed. "You just took me by surprise at dinner. I didn't expect you to act like we were on the verge of breaking up...I just thought you'd let me tell them later."

"I wanted to be convincing," she told him again. "I wanted it to look like we'd had a fight, and that I was obviously annoyed with you. That way they'll believe it when we split."

"Yeah, well I'm sure they bought it. But now what do we do? I can't even believe they want us to go to Peppertown." He shuddered.

"I don't know. It doesn't sound all that bad." And it hadn't. That Adam had made the offer in the first place still blew her mind. Maybe he didn't think she was some trashy woman. Maybe he'd decided to trust her.

Nate stared at her in disbelief. "Are you serious? I thought you were just amusing my mom back there."

"No. I wasn't at all. I could really use a vacation, Nate. And I don't know the next time I'll get such a great offer," she said bluntly.

"But it's *Peppertown*."

"It's still a vacation. Besides, I've always wanted to learn how to milk a cow."

"More like milk my brother," he grumbled.

Christy's cheeks warmed, her blood pressure rose. "Stop it. I don't deserve those nasty little comments. After all I've done for you? Besides, so what if it is to see Adam. Tomorrow the charade is over."

"But you're going to be staying with my family." He was obviously surprised. "You still want to break up? It'd be a little weird if you were my ex-girlfriend and staying with them."

"Well..." Shit. She hadn't thought that far ahead. "Why don't we just say we're taking some time apart. Seeing other people or something?"

"Time apart. Considering a break up?"

"Sure."

"That could work. And you don't even have to tell my parents."

"Well, I'm telling Adam," she said firmly.

Nate hesitated, and then nodded.

"And maybe when you meet up with us on Friday or Saturday we could do the breaking up bit."

She really wanted this week with Adam. To be able to put aside the guilt and enjoy the country boy back on his own turf.

"That just might work." Nate gave her a considering look.

"Are you sure you want to do this, though? It would mean spending five days alone with my family."

"I wouldn't be here discussing this if I wasn't okay with it. I love your family, Nate, I wish you would too. They're great people."

"Lord, she's been brainwashed."

"I think they'll be a lot more understanding than you think when you tell them."

"I'll let you know how that goes when I do. But trust me it's not going to be a Cinderella story."

Christy shook her head with a sigh. It was actually pretty sad. Of course it wasn't going to be easy when he came out to his family, but he'd be a hell of a lot happier in the end.

"Will you call your parents tonight and let them know I'll be driving over tomorrow?"

"Sure. Check your email and I'll send you the directions and their phone number." Nate paused. "They're going to be so excited that you're coming, Christy. You know, they really love you. Maybe it wouldn't be such a bad thing for you to get together with Adam."

Her heart sped up as she stared at him. "You told me Adam just loves women, and it's just about getting laid for him."

"Well most men eventually settle down. They just have to meet the one woman who makes them want to," Nate pointed out. "How many fifty or sixty-year-old players do you see running around? Very few. And I'm not counting famous men in Hollywood, because that's not reality."

"I'm just not so sure Adam is this insatiable sex prowler that you seem to think he is in the first place."

"You could be right, maybe he's changed. I'm just going by what I used to see." Nate let go of the door and dug into his pocket for his keys. "I'll call my parents, email you, and see you Saturday afternoon."

"Sounds like a plan."

As she was driving home, Christy couldn't help but think about what he'd said about Adam. But what if he was wrong? If her instincts were wrong? Maybe Adam was just toying with her. Having fun and amusing himself. Going after what he thought he couldn't have.

She shook her head to clear the heavy thoughts. There was more between them, she could feel it. And this next week together would prove it.

Chapter Ten

Early Monday morning Christy drove through the mountain pass, a cappuccino in her right hand as she steered with her left.

She'd stayed up until midnight as she packed, going through her closet to figure out what to bring. She'd had to dig through her dresser until, by some miracle, she'd found a pair of old jeans. It'd been so long since she'd worn any, she pretty much lived in skirts.

What did one wear in the country anyway? She'd decided to stick with her girly-girl roots and put on a denim skirt with a pink T-shirt that said *Dancing Queen* on it.

I'm doing it. She was actually heading over the mountains to farm country. Republican land, as Nate was so fond of calling it. Who knew what awaited her there. Maybe she really would milk a cow. Or farm things. Whatever that entailed.

She glanced at the clock on her dashboard and wiped a bead of sweat off her forehead. It was only ten in the morning and she was already sweating. And it was just going to get worse once she was on the other side of the mountains. The heat on average could be ten to fifteen degrees hotter. No matter, she could take it.

Or not. An hour later she admitted defeat. The heat was miserable, stifling, and just plain unbearable.

Damn her stupid apartment, she cursed silently. If she hadn't insisted on living in that run-down piece of junk, she could have afforded a new car. A car with air conditioning. Oh God, air conditioning sounded better than sex with Adam right about now.

"I would sell my soul for air conditioning!" She moaned and stuck her arm out the window to try to create a breeze. It didn't help. And then a bug smashed into her hand.

"Oh, ick!" She dragged her hand back inside and grabbed a napkin from her glove compartment, wiping down the small mess now covering her arm.

She tossed the napkin into the back of the car just as her cell phone rang. Christy scrambled to find it, surprised she even had reception out here.

She flipped it open. "Hello?"

"Are you thinking about me?"

"Hmm. Maybe I am, cowboy. Are you going to ask me what I'm wearing now?" Christy grinned as she balanced the phone between her shoulder and her ear.

Adam's slow laughter drifted through the line, making her hot in an entirely different way. "Now that sounds like a great idea. What are you wearing, darlin'?"

"A skirt. A shirt."

"And underneath?"

Christy grinned and couldn't resist teasing him. "A bra with holes for my nipples and crotchless panties."

There was silence on the other line, and she burst out laughing.

"I'm kidding, Adam."

"I wish you weren't. You have no idea how hard you just got me."

"Trust me, I have an idea." She squirmed in her seat, her panties growing wet as she thought about the other night in his truck. "Maybe we should do some shopping for that kind of thing when I arrive."

"Unfortunately, Peppertown doesn't have too many of those shops. Where are you anyway?"

"Just passing through Ellensburg. I've been forced to listen to country music for the last hour. Once I got over the pass, all the radio stations suddenly became country. Funny how that works."

"Nice. Hear anything you like?"

"Well, there was some song about a man who chose fishing over his woman, and then another where some chick is bragging about being a redneck." Christy laughed. "I'll tell you one thing, country music can be pretty funny."

"Glad you like it. I just wanted to check on you. You got my number, right?"

"It's in my phone now that you called me."

"Okay. I can't wait to see you, Christy. Just give me a ring if you need me."

"Will do." Christy closed her phone and tried to ignore the fluttery sensation in her belly. He'd called her Christy. He never called her Christy, it was always *darlin'*. And the way he'd said he couldn't wait to see her...

They'd turned a corner. Somehow it had been decided—without actual words—that they were going to stop avoiding what was happening between them. Thank God. Because she hated the idea of trying to hold out when she'd be so close to Adam for the week.

When she was just outside of Peppertown, her car started to overheat. The little stick on the meter started creeping up towards the "H". Should she pull over or keep driving? Finally, she just pulled over.

It wasn't so bad was it? There wasn't any smoke pouring out from under her hood, which would actually happen every now and then. She sat and watched the minutes tick by. When it had been fifteen, she started the engine again. The gage hovered above the medium line and didn't move any higher. Might as well try to make it to Adam's parents.

Their place wasn't hard to find. And just like Nate had described in the email, their farm was painted white with green trim.

Christy pulled her Beetle—which was starting to overheat again—into their dirt driveway and turned off her car. She opened the door and stepped out, taking a moment to enjoy the fresh, untainted air and the mild breeze.

Candace came running out of the house. "You made it!" she cried, hurrying down the porch stairs and across the lawn. "How was your drive, dear?"

"All right." Christy's breath whooshed from her body as Candace smothered her in a big hug. "My car started to overheat, but it—"

"Oh no! Adam will take a look at it. Oops. I'll be right back, dear. I forgot I have a pie in the oven." Candace released her and hurried back into the house.

Jeez, that woman was a riot. Christy watched her run back inside. Then her gaze drifted to the corner of the porch and that's when she saw him.

Adam leaned against the railing with an iced drink in his hand and watched her. He straightened and started walking towards her.

"What's this about your car?"

Tempting Adam

She swallowed hard as his lazy stride brought him closer to her. Before she realized what she was doing, Christy had reached out and snatched the glass from his hands.

"Do you mind?" Without waiting for an answer, Christy downed the rest of his drink. Her tongue flicked out over her lips to absorb the few sweet and tangy drops that had trickled down her mouth. "I assume this is Adam's Apple cider?"

"You assume right," Adam drawled as he used his thumb to wipe away another drop from her chin. His gaze heated. "Do you like it?"

"I love it." His touch had her shivering despite the heat. "It's sweet and refreshing. Just what I needed after that drive over the mountains."

"No air conditioning in your vintage Beetle, huh?" He glanced at her car. "You didn't answer me about your car. What's wrong with it?"

"Just overheating a bit." She swished the glass to help the ice melt, and then swallowed another sip. "It happens all the time, don't worry about it."

The frown on his face indicated that he definitely *was* going to worry about it. Christy didn't want him to have to shoulder that extra responsibility, but was oddly pleased that he'd decided to do it anyway.

"Would you help me carry in my bags?"

"No." He stopped her from reaching into her backseat to pull out her two gym bags. "You're not going to be staying with my parents."

"Oh. I thought I was." Christy glanced down at his hand that now covered her wrist and her heart pounded. "I must have heard wrong. Where's the nearest motel, I can check into a room—"

139

"No." He stepped closer to her. "I want you to check into my house."

Adam watched both surprise and desire flicker in her gaze. Her lips parted and her body swayed towards him—it was all he could do to not bend down and kiss her.

"You were supposed to stay with my parents," he explained. God he wanted to kiss her—right now. But with his parents just inside the house it wasn't such a good idea. "It turns out that their spare room isn't available due to a termite problem. They asked if I wouldn't mind taking you in."

Her eyes widened. "Are you sure you don't mind? I can get a motel if you'd rather—"

"Christy." His voice was low and rough. "Make no mistake about it. I want you to stay with me."

A flush made its way up her neck and through her cheeks, and her mouth curved into a lazy seductive smile.

"Are you okay with that?" He needed to make sure they were in the same boat.

"I'm..." she hesitated and then nodded, "...I'm more than okay with that."

She'd be in his house tonight. Maybe in his bed. The thought almost made him go instantly hard. "That's just what I was hoping to hear."

"So what's the plan for now?"

"My parents want us to come over later for dinner. But for now, why don't we grab your stuff and throw it in my truck. I don't want you driving any more than you need to."

Christy rolled her eyes, but didn't argue as he plucked the two bags from the backseat of her Beetle.

"Anything else?" He looked around for the rest of her stuff.

"Nope, that's it." She smiled. "I'm a light packer. One bag is full of clothes, makeup and toiletry items."

"And the other?"

"Lingerie."

This time his dick did go hard. "Kidding again?"

"Nope." She tilted her head and offered him a suggestive glance. "I like to wear sexy things on the parts of my body that no one else can see. Well, unless I let them see."

And apparently she was going to let him see. Adam thought back on the red lingerie from the first night they'd been together and gave a silent groan.

He set her bags in the back of his pickup and then turned back to face her. "Why don't we say goodbye to my parents before we go back to my place."

"Good call. I haven't even said hi to your dad yet." Christy followed him towards the front door.

Adam led her inside and immediately spotted his dad sitting in a recliner in the living room. An untouched sandwich rested on a plate on his lap, as he stared at the newscast on the television.

"Dad, Christy arrived a few minutes ago."

His dad looked up in surprise. He looked tired as he pushed himself to his feet, setting the plate on the table next to him.

"Christy, glad you could make it over, young lady."

Christy slipped into the hug his dad offered with ease.

"Thank you, Steven. I'm glad to be here. It was so sweet that you guys even thought to invite me."

"We wanted you to visit us, dear." His mom came out of the kitchen with an apron around her waist. "I was just finishing up getting some things ready for dinner tonight. Do you like fried chicken, Christy?"

"I love fried chicken."

"Wonderful. This is an old homemade recipe and I hope you'll love it." She glanced quickly at Adam. "Did Adam tell you that we had to move you in with him instead?"

"He mentioned it, yes. That's fine. I don't really mind where I stay. I'm just excited to be here."

"I feel plain awful about this." His mom cleared her throat and lowered her gaze. "Here I invite you out to spend the week with us and we end up with termites. Can you believe our luck?"

"That is pretty bad luck," Christy admitted with a smile. "I hope it's not too complex to get rid of."

"Well, Steven says he knows what to do." She rolled her eyes. "But you know men. I keep telling him to call the people who do this for a living."

"Good gravy, woman. I know what I'm doing," his dad piped up from his chair. "Will you let me take care of it, instead of—"

"All right, all right." His mom waved her hands, winked at Adam and Christy, and walked back into the kitchen. "I'll see you both tonight."

"Thank you, Candace," Christy called after her.

Adam turned back to face her, wondering if she thought his family was nuts. And the strange thing was he hadn't seen any evidence of a termite problem.

"You ready to head over to my place?"

"Sure. See you later, Steven." Christy waved goodbye to his dad and then they left the house.

Christy began. "So your parents run a farm. Does that mean that they raise all their own animals?"

"Some." Adam shot her a glance. "Why?"

"Well," she hesitated. "I like meat, don't get me wrong, but did she…is that chicken something she just went out back and killed?"

Adam threw his head back and gave a long hard laugh. "Heck, no. Mom can't even kill a spider. We never did that kind of farming—we were always more into the agriculture side."

"Good. It's just so much easier to eat meat when you've bought it in the meat department at the grocery store. But if I had to think about it running around in the backyard before it became dinner, then it just changes the whole thing."

Adam shook his head with amusement. *Better to not inform her that the chicken had come from their neighbor's farm.* Christy smiled up at him and then said, "Anyway, I think your parents are adorable."

So she didn't think they were nuts. "Thanks, I'm partial to them. How are yours?" Adam asked as they climbed into his truck.

"My mom is fantastic. But I haven't seen my dad since I was five."

Adam gave a surprised glance. "Really now? Why's that?"

"He was one of those guys who just didn't want to be a dad." She shrugged. "He did the occasional visit for the first five years of my life, but then kind of gave up trying to pretend he cared."

"Was your mom ever married to him?"

"No. They met at a party in college—both of them were just nineteen when my mom got pregnant."

"I'm sorry. That can't have been easy on you," Adam said, not sure what else to say. His childhood hadn't been without its problems, but he'd had a well-rounded family life growing up.

"I won't lie, it was hard at times. But it's not like I'm the only kid who grew up without a dad," she replied, her gaze turned out the window. "And Mom more than made up for the fact. She's amazing. You'll have to meet her sometime."

"I'd like to." Adam turned his truck off onto his street. "There's my place."

Christy's gaze returned straight ahead and she gasped. It wasn't an uncommon reaction when someone first saw his place.

The house itself was a two-story, early-twentieth-century home, fixed up and painted a dark shade of blue with white trim. It was set on thirty acres of land, and beside the house there was a large pond—almost a small lake—with a short dock and rowboat at the end.

"This is gorgeous." Christy's voice told him just how awed she was. "How did you...did you fix up the house yourself?"

"This was my first real purchase after Adam's Apples got off the ground." His gaze scanned his home with pride. *God he loved it here.* "Once I knew I'd made it, I wanted a real nice place of my own."

"You found it. And you made it beautiful."

His chest swelled with pride. It had been important somehow, that she liked his home. Why was that so important? This wasn't like him. He sure was going to have to watch himself this week. Otherwise he might do something stupid. Like beg her to ditch Nate for good and...and what? *Don't go there. Not now.*

Hell, he already felt like the biggest asshole on the earth for all the things he wanted to do to his brother's girlfriend. Had done to her. He shouldn't have invited her over for the week, but hell, the thought of not bringing her here had been more painful than the guilt.

After he parked the truck, she climbed out and walked

across his property towards the dock. Adam waited, watching her for a moment, then climbed out and followed her.

Christy slid her sunglasses over her eyes, heading straight for the lake. She was completely in love with his home, and she hadn't even been inside yet.

The heat stroked down on her, causing her shirt to stick to her back as she walked out onto the dock.

"I could go for a swim right now," she told Adam as he came up behind her.

The lake was small, probably part of his property. At the other end there was a small gathering of trees but no other houses around.

"Maybe later we will."

Adam's hands settled on her hips, and a tremor moved through her. He turned her to face him, his muscular thighs and hips pressed snugly against her.

"I'm glad you like it, darlin'. And I'm glad you're here."

His head dipped to kiss her and Christy's eyes fluttered shut. She tilted her face up to meet him halfway and his lips covered hers. Soft and gentle. He traced her lower lip with his tongue before delving inside and deepening the kiss.

Everything melted inside her. It felt so right to be with him. To touch him.

Her tongue moved against his, harder. Faster. And the kiss turned from being sweet to something a lot more sinful and needy. All of a sudden her body wasn't just wet from perspiration, but she was damp in areas the sun never even touched. It had nothing to do with the heat outside, but the heat of the man who held her.

Adam finally broke away, his breathing ragged as he

touched his forehead to hers.

"Well, damn. That felt too good to be wrong."

"It's not wrong." She slipped her head onto his shoulder, wrapping her arms around his waist. *Time to alleviate some of that guilt Adam carried.*

"No?"

"No. Nate and I are taking some time apart. So whatever guilt you're having, trash it. Now. This week is about us."

He was silent for a moment. "Time apart?"

Too bad her head was on his shoulder, because she would have loved to see the expression on his face. There'd been something in his tone when he'd said that. But was it good or bad?

"Yes, time apart. So that means we can get as frisky as we want to, and no one needs to pack their bags for a guilt trip." She pulled away and looked up at him. His gaze held a bit of relief.

"Come on, let me show you the house," he said, his voice more gruff. "Get you settled in your room."

He grabbed her hand and led her away from the lake.

Her room. Did that mean they wouldn't be sharing one together? Was he changing his mind about her?

No. That kiss. That kiss had been hot. But...she didn't understand him. Not at all. Maybe he was still hung up about the idea of her and Nate. Though she really had thought that the whole *we're taking time apart* bit would appease him.

Don't rush things. Disappointment threatened to rear its head, but she pushed it away. They had a week together. An entire week. Besides, they might have separate rooms, but that didn't mean she wouldn't end up in his bed.

Adam led her inside of the house, the hardwood floors

creaking beneath her feet. It was just as beautiful inside as out. There was a spiral staircase that led up to the second floor. Antique furniture, handmade curtains, plants...not exactly the furnishings she would have expected for a bachelor pad.

Her gaze landed on the chaise lounge. "Oh my God. I can't believe you have one of these." She ran over and sprawled on the red velvet.

Adam's gaze followed her. "Very sexy."

"I think so." She tossed her hands above her head and stretched, arching her body. Her breasts thrust higher into the air. "I always see these things and think of a parlor in a house of pleasure."

Adam shifted, his gaze intent on her breasts. "If you stay lying like that for much longer, this certainly will turn into a house of pleasure."

Christy laughed. "Is that a promise?"

Her heart skipped a beat as he sat down next to her, his fingertips trailing over her ribcage and towards the swell of her breast.

Christy bit her lip, anticipating the coming contact. *Just a little higher.* He curled his fingers under the swell of her breast, cupping her fully in his palm. She closed her eyes. *That's it.* His thumb did a quick sweep of her nipple and it immediately tightened, almost painfully.

"You are so responsive." His thumb stroked again.

"Mmm." She opened her eyes, just a bit to look at him. "You make it easy to be."

He lifted his hand from her. *No.* She sighed with frustration. What now? Why wouldn't he touch her?

"I really should show you your room."

Her room? Why? Unless they were going to be having crazy

sex in her room, she really didn't care. Why did he keep getting her all worked up and then stop. It was like the adult version of *Red Light, Green Light*. Only the red lights were a lot more maddening this time around.

Sliding off of the couch, she followed him up the winding staircase. The room he brought her into was beautiful. Again, it seemed a little odd for a guy.

The queen-sized bed was in the middle of the room against the wall, and the canopy above it was draped with sheer white curtains. The bed itself was neatly made and covered with a pretty quilt stitched with various pastel patterns.

In fact the whole room was done in pastel coloring that seemed to match the antique theme of the house.

"This is a woman's room," she said, turning to him with a curious glance.

"It's my guest room."

"And I suppose your guests are women?"

"Not really. My mom actually came over and fixed it up for you."

"Ah." She turned back to look around. That made more sense. His mom had great taste. "Do you mind if I open the window? It's a little hot in here."

"I'll get it for you." He crossed the room and slid it open. "I have portable fans in all the rooms if you want one. Yours is in the closet, do you want me to get it?"

"I'm all right for now." She paused. "Although, I am a little tired after that long drive. Do you mind if I catch a quick nap before we go to your parents' for dinner?"

"Now that sounds like a great idea. Are you sure you don't want some lunch first?"

"I had a breakfast sandwich and a cappuccino a couple of

hours ago. I'm good to go."

"All right, darlin'. Just let me know if you need anything."

You know exactly what I need. "Okay."

He turned, smiling at her one last time before leaving her alone in the room.

Christy scowled. Yeah, he knew what she needed. But apparently he wasn't ready to help her out with that right now.

Christy walked to the door and closed it most of the way, leaving it open a crack to let the air circulate. Then she turned back and glanced at the bed.

And if he wasn't going to help her out, that was fine. Pulling off her skirt, Christy climbed onto the bed in just her T-shirt and bikini panties.

Nope. She didn't need him. She'd just take matters into her own hands.

Adam fiddled around downstairs in the kitchen. Lord. She was upstairs. Christy was upstairs. Lying in his spare bedroom. In bed.

God, how he wanted her. And obviously she wanted him. So why was he being such a goddamn idiot? Why wasn't he upstairs with her?

He opened the fridge and grabbed himself a beer—there was only so much apple cider he could drink a day. He took a sip, before going to sit down in the living room in the rocker.

This was crazy. What was he trying to prove to himself? That he didn't *have* to have her? Was he trying to prove to himself that he could resist her? *Yes.*

He'd never wanted a woman this bad. So strong that it consumed him. Made him damn near stupid.

To want a woman beyond rational thought was ridiculous—

not to mention unusual for him. In fact, it had never happened before. There'd always been a little leftover self-control.

But not with Christy. She sucked him dry of all self-control. The memory of what happened in the truck ran through his head. *Shit.*

He wanted to run upstairs, tear off that ridiculous *Dancing Queen* shirt she was wearing, and make love to her until she was cross-eyed.

Which is exactly why he couldn't. Maybe it was stupid, but he needed that last amount of restraint. To be able to know that he still had some self-control. Even if it was the tiniest thread.

And then there was still Nate. Of course, Christy had just told him they were taking some time apart, but still. Maybe he should give Nate a call and find out his side of the story. Hell, maybe he ought to just confess. Admit that Christy was the fire in his blood.

Yeah. Calling Nate was probably the decent thing to do.

Adam kicked his feet up on the footrest and closed his eyes. The room was quiet except for the stereo which was turned on low, playing an old Garth Brooks song.

He had just started to doze off when he heard it. His eyelids snapped open and he went still. What *was* that?

But the house was quiet again except for the light background music.

He stood up. No, he'd definitely heard something. It had come from upstairs and had sounded like a strangled groan.

Peppertown was a small town, but that didn't mean it didn't have a crime rate. He moved up the stairs, keeping his steps light. It wasn't likely he'd find anyone up there besides Christy, but it didn't hurt to make sure. She was probably just having a bad dream in her sleep.

Her door was open a crack and he pushed on it slightly. Adam stuck his head around the opening in the door and glanced at the bed.

Sweet Jesus!

Chapter Eleven

Christy lay on the bed with her fingers inside her white lace panties, her body writhing as she stroked herself.

Leave and shut the door. Even though Adam ordered himself to move, his body wasn't following any orders made by his brain. His dick throbbed to life as Christy groaned again, and her fingers disappeared even deeper inside her panties. He could smell her arousal, even from across the room.

God, he just wanted to fling open the door and jump into bed with her. But watching her, seeing her pleasure herself was just as hot.

She bit her lip, maybe in an effort to keep silent or because the pleasure was so intense. Suddenly her body started to shake, and then her toes curled. Her hips arched into the air as her breath came out on an almost silent gasp, before she collapsed onto the bed.

Christ. Adam just managed not to groan.

Her breathing was heavy as she rolled over onto her stomach, pushing her enticing round ass into the air.

He ground his teeth together and pulled back from the doorway. He tried to get back downstairs as quietly as he'd come up.

Now how in the hell was he going to get through the rest of the day with that arousing vision in his head?

Christy sat beside Adam at dinner. She glanced at him again, for about the tenth time in the last five minutes. But still he didn't acknowledge her. In fact he'd been avoiding eye contact almost all afternoon. Why was that?

Maybe she hadn't imagined the light footsteps outside her room early today. Right after she'd given herself the well-needed orgasm.

Hmm...had Adam watched her masturbate? Interesting. Somehow, the idea wasn't so embarrassing. In fact, it was pretty much a turn on. She shifted in her seat. *Do not get all hot and bothered at the family dinner!*

"This chicken is wonderful, Candace. You simply have to give me the recipe." Christy took another bite of her crispy drumstick, chewing the meat slowly. "And the potatoes, oh my gosh. Forget cider, you should open a restaurant."

Adam's gaze shot to her, the glare on his face amusing. Apparently he didn't appreciate her humor. He sure was irritable tonight.

"I'm so glad you like it, dear." Candace smiled. "Adam usually loves it, too, but he's barely touched his food tonight. Are you feeling all right, dear?"

"I'm fine."

Funny, but his curt voice indicated he was anything but fine. Christy hid a smile. Maybe her big cowboy was just the tiniest bit sexually frustrated? Well good. He'd had every chance to take out his frustration on her, but for some unknown reason had decided not to.

"Well, save some room," Steven added. "Candace made pie for dessert."

"I love pie." Christy licked a biscuit crumb from her finger. "It wouldn't happen to be blueberry, would it?"

Adam's glare intensified and he mumbled something under his breath. Had he sworn? She could have sworn he'd said the F-word under his breath.

"Apple, dear. We're an apple family." Candace stood up and carried her plate into the kitchen. "I'll start doing the dishes."

"I'll help." Christy dropped the rest of her chicken onto the plate and picked it up. "Can I get yours, Adam? Or are you still working it? I mean working on it."

His mouth drew tighter and he pushed his plate towards her without responding. Christy balanced it on top her own, before turning to take Steven's empty plate as well.

She joined Candace in the kitchen. Christy rinsed and dried the dishes as Candace washed them. It was so cute, the Youngs were just so old-fashioned. They probably air dried their laundry on a clothesline, too.

Adam had obviously been raised to be a perfect gentleman. He'd impressed her from day one in the coffee shop, and then on the dance floor. In the bedroom he was incredible. Her cheeks flushed as she thought about that night in his truck. This week alone with Adam would be wonderful. No Nate to stroll along and screw things up.

"How's my son, Christy?"

Christy smiled. "Wonderful."

"You're happy together?"

"I've never been this happy—" she broke off. *Hello, idiot!* Candace was talking about Nate, not Adam.

Oh, God. Christy's body went rigid. What had she just

done? She was supposed to be preparing them for a breakup, not praising her relationship with Nate. Why? Why couldn't she take back her words? Or maybe just point out she'd been referring to the other son. Yeah, neither was going to happen right now.

"I'm so glad that you feel that way about him," Candace said, her tone light. "I do hope some day you marry my son. I couldn't ask for a better daughter-in-law."

"*Daughter-in-law?*" Christy yelped

"What?" Adam—who'd just walked into the kitchen—spoke at the same time.

"Oh," Candace waved a dish rag in the air. "I'm just speaking as a hopeful mother. Unless there's something I don't know?"

"Of course not. Nate and I aren't getting married."

Adam gave her a suspicious glance as he walked to the fridge and pulled two sodas out. She shook her head at him, trying to communicate silently. *You heard wrong!*

"Oh, I know that, dear." Candace smiled and went back to washing the dishes.

Adam didn't look happy, his jaw was tight as he shut the fridge and walked past her back into the living room.

Oh, God. Hopefully he wasn't giving too much weight to what his mom had just said. Christy sighed. She'd been making so much progress with him. Had finally gotten him to trust her.

The last thing she needed was for them to go back to square one. But maybe she was just overreacting. Because he couldn't hide that other look in his eyes. The look that said he wanted nothing more than to bend her over the table and push up her skirt.

"So, Christy, did you like Adam's home?"

Christy replaced her previous visual with the memory of Adam's house. "It's absolutely beautiful. I love it."

"Wonderful. I really want you to enjoy your stay while you're here. I did up your room. Did he mention that?"

"He did, yes. It looks beautiful. You're quite the interior designer, Candace."

Candace giggled and waved the dishrag her way. "Oh, it was nothing. You should tell Adam to show you around town. There's a nice little bar on Main Street that I think you'd enjoy."

"We'll have to see what he's up for. I'll make sure he takes me there one of the nights this week."

An hour later they'd all eaten pie, and Steven was asleep in his recliner. Christy and Adam said their goodbyes to Candace, and then walked outside to Adam's truck.

"What's the plan now?" Christy asked. "Your mom said you should take me to the bar on Main Street."

"Are you up for the bar on Main Street?" His lips curled as he gave her a quick glance. "Hey, I have an even better idea."

Oh...so now he wanted to do the whole sex thing. Well, better late than never. "Whatever it is, I'm up for it."

"You're sure?"

"I'm sure."

"All right, darlin', you asked for it."

Christy mentally reviewed her choices of lingerie. Which one to choose. The red one? No, she'd already done that. Maybe the black. Oh, yeah, black was sexy. Or—hey. How come they'd just driven past his house?

"We're not going back to your place?"

"Nope."

"Oh." She bit her lip. Maybe he was taking her to the local

makeout spot. Hmm, there went the lingerie. Ah, well, not like it really mattered.

Adam turned the car down a small road, and a second later a small barn loomed ahead of them.

A roll in the hay. Oh, perfect. A total fantasy of hers!

Christy got out of the truck, already envisioning the torrid sex in a barn they were about to have.

But as they approached the door to the barn she heard the music. Adam grinned down at her, before swinging open the door and gesturing her inside.

Why do I get the feeling we're not here for sex? Christy stepped past him into the barn. Oh God. Not this. Anything but this.

Country music blared as hoards of couples moved on the dance floor. And they were two-stepping.

She should have guessed. Especially when Adam pulled out a cowboy hat from the back of his truck and put it on. Ah well, if it couldn't be sex, then at least it was dancing.

"You ever done this kind of dancing?" Adam glanced at her as they made their way through the crowd.

"I can't say that I have." The dancing going on around them moved a mile a minute. Her mind raced to keep up with the steps.

"Well, tonight you're going to learn." He took her hand and dragged her onto the floor. "After all, you taught me Salsa on your territory. So I figure I should teach you how we dance 'round these parts."

It didn't look anything like Salsa, but she gave him her best confident smile. "Let's do it."

"Hold on tight, darlin'," Adam murmured in her ear. "Payback's a bitch."

And it was, she thought after they'd been spinning and stomping for an hour. She was sweaty, tired, but even still, having the time of her life.

"I need a break."

Christy moaned with relief as Adam led them off the floor. In the corner of the barn were chairs, tables, and a cooler full of Budweiser and bottled water. Adam went straight to it and grabbed them both a beer.

Christy snagged a chair and sat down, grateful for the moment off her feet. The smell of hay and sweat was in the air, the sound of laughter and music rang throughout the barn. It was so different than what she was used to. But not in a bad way.

"What do you think?" Adam asked, sitting down beside her and talking a hard swig from his bottle.

"I love it," Christy admitted, grinning at him. "Once I get the hang of it a little more, I'm sure you'll have to drag me off the floor instead of the other way around."

"I have to say, darlin', you did a lot better than I thought you would. You're just a plain old good dancer. Doesn't matter what you're doing."

"Thanks. You're sweet." She lowered her lashes. God, she could've visually devoured him all night long. With the tight jeans, white T-shirt, and cowboy hat, he certainly fit the cowboy image. And looked damn fine in it too.

"Adam Young. I didn't know you'd gotten back in town."

Christy's gaze snapped back up at the sound of the sultry, high-pitched voice. The woman standing in front of them was tall, centerfold-curvaceous, with long red hair and appraising brown eyes. Eyes that were taking in Adam. Apparently Christy wasn't the only one who thought Adam looked damn near edible.

"I just got back yesterday." Adam gave the woman a slow smile. "Mandy Lou Davis, I'd like to introduce you to Christy Wallace."

Mandy Lou? Christy wrinkled her nose. *People actually named their kid Mandy Lou?*

When Mandy looked over at her, her gaze showed that she didn't care much for Christy either.

"Now, don't tell me you brought yourself home a girlfriend from Seattle, Adam?" Mandy asked, keeping her hostile gaze on Christy.

Damn. Christy's mouth tightened as she prepared for the inevitable response from Adam.

"Actually, she's Nate's girlfriend."

"Nate's girlfriend?" Her expression changed abruptly to surprise. "But I always thought that Nate...hmm. Interesting. Well anyway, Christy. If you're Nate's girlfriend, it's nice to meet you."

"But only if I'm *Nate's* girlfriend?"

"Well, of course." Mandy Lou leaned over and pulled Adam's hat off his head, then settled it on her own tumbled waves. "You can be anyone's. Just as long as you're not Adam's."

Bitch! Christy took a swig of beer so the word wouldn't slip past her lips. *Could the woman be any more obvious?*

"I've got what you might call a little crush on Adam, don't I, sweet cheeks?" Mandy reached down to rub his shoulders.

Okay, apparently she could be a lot more obvious. Christy just managed to restrain herself from slapping the other woman's hands.

"You wanna take me out on the floor for a spin?" Mandy asked.

Adam glanced at Christy. His grin was wide, and there was laughter in his eyes. *Ugh.* He thought this was funny? And why was he looking at her? It wasn't like he was going to ask for her permission. Technically Christy had no claim on him. Nada. Zilch. He was single and available.

"I've got a beer, *y'all* go and have fun," Christy drawled, not bothering to hide her sarcasm.

Adam's smile widened. Great, if he hadn't already known that she was jealous, she'd just pretty much declared it.

She clenched her fingers around the beer as they moved onto the dance floor and started sashaying around. They looked good together. Actually, they were probably the most talented couple on the floor.

Physically, they were a striking pair. Both tall and good-looking. Mandy came to his chin, whereas Christy had to tilt her head up to even see it.

Easy girl, Christy told herself. Getting this worked up over a man who wasn't even hers was just ridiculous.

"I'd offer to buy you a beer, but they're free."

Christy glanced up at the man who'd just come to stand beside her.

"And the fact that I already have one?" She tilted the neck of her bottle at him.

He wasn't too bad-looking—a little more beefy than she was used to. Kind of had that whole football linebacker bulk going on, and maybe the mentality of one who'd taken too many hits to the head.

"Yeah, but you're almost done with it."

"So I am." She downed the rest and tossed the bottle in a nearby barrel full of other empty bottles.

"Tell you what, little lady." He giggled—actually giggled.

"And you are little. I can get you another beer, or we can dance. Do either of those sound good to you?"

Not really. But then watching Mandy Lou and Adam circle the floor like freaking homecoming royalty wasn't a much better option.

"We can dance."

So, how much was she going to regret this? He grabbed her wrist, almost dragging her onto the dance floor. If he lifted her off the ground at any time and attempted to carry her, it was over.

"So, you're not from around here, are you?"

"I'm from Seattle," she replied as they found a place in-between couples.

He draped a meaty arm around her waist and held her hand with his free one. When his fingers started moving up her ribs, she accidentally stepped on his foot with her high heel.

"Sorry." *Yeah right.*

"About what?"

God, was his foot so big that he hadn't even felt that? She'd have to try harder next time.

"What's your name, little lady?"

"Not little lady, that's for sure."

"I like you, you're kind of funny."

When Christy looked up at him, he was smiling and she noticed he was missing a few important teeth. Score one for the too many hits in football theory.

"You got a boyfriend?"

"No. And I'm not looking, thanks."

"So are you one of them girls just looking for sex then?"

"Uh, tempting as that may be, I'm gonna have to say no."

She gave a shudder of disgust. Weren't country boys supposed to be all polite and gentleman-like?

"Well, I guess we can just dance then."

"I guess so." Christy shot another loathing glance at Adam and Mandy Lou.

Good Lord, could Mandy Lou get any closer to Adam? They didn't need to be that close. It was like they were lovers or something.

The thought stuck. *Had* they been lovers?

The way the other woman was gazing up at him, and giggling as they danced around the barn...it wouldn't surprise her if they had. Maybe at one point at least. Interesting. She would have to keep a closer eye on those two.

Chapter Twelve

Adam was only half listening to the words that poured out of Mandy Lou's mouth. They never amounted to much in any case. Mostly just how good they'd be together.

Mandy Lou had never made it a secret that she was after his hide. Had been since fifth grade and they were in Mrs. Lupe's class. One day at recess she'd shown him hers, and he'd shown her his. From then on she'd declared herself in love with him, and he'd just been in love with women in general.

Although they'd never dated, so to speak, he had made the mistake of sleeping with her. It was after a friend's wedding a few years ago, and they'd both been drunk. And now Mandy Lou had it in her mind to go after him even more so. He shouldn't really even be dancing with her right now. But, hell, he couldn't resist getting Christy all riled. Especially after the hell she'd put him through at dinner.

So, no, he wasn't really paying attention to the chatty woman dancing with him. His focus was much more centered on the woman across the room who now danced in Bubba Jenkins' arms.

Adam's jaw clenched. He didn't like the way Bubba was leering down at Christy, like she was chicken fried steak and he'd like to be the gravy covering her.

"I swear you haven't heard a word I've said, Adam Young."

"I'm listening, Mandy." He didn't take his eyes off Christy.

"You sure? You seem more interested in your brother's girlfriend."

Adam's annoyance jacked up another level. He was having a real hard time being polite to Mandy, and not cross the room and drag Christy away from Bubba's grasp. What had she been thinking by agreeing to dance with him? She couldn't be enjoying it. And the way her lips were stretched into a grim smile he could see he was right.

"You'll have to excuse me, Mandy." He moved them to the edge of the dance floor and then released her, grabbing his hat back.

She started to argue with him, but he was already halfway across the floor to retrieve Christy.

Just in time. Bubba's hand skimmed up her side as he attempted to cop a feel of her breast. Christy's heeled foot smashed down on Bubba's foot. Bubba glanced down more in surprise than in pain, but it gave her a moment to slide out of his grasp.

"Having fun, darlin'?" Adam asked as they met up a few seconds later in the corner of the room.

"Oh, just a *charming* time."

Yeah, she seemed a little worked up.

"I see you met Bubba. He's a great dancer, don't you think?" He couldn't resist teasing her a little.

"Now why doesn't it surprise me that the town's mammoth pervert is named Bubba?"

"Is Bubba a pervert?" Adam shook his head and put a look of wonder on his face. "Huh, I never would have figured."

Christy shot him a fierce glance that said she didn't believe in his ignorance for a moment.

"I wouldn't have had to dance with Bubba if you hadn't gone off and left me alone."

"I'm missing something." Adam shook his head. "Because I danced with someone, you had to?"

"Yes." She sighed. "Okay, fine. I didn't want to stand on the sidelines looking like an idiot while you waltzed around with the prom queen."

"Three things. One, we were two-stepping, not waltzing. I can't waltz. Two, Mandy was never prom queen, but I think she did win some kind of corn pageant one year."

"Never mind." Christy turned away from him, heading straight for the exit. "I don't want to hear it."

"And three," he went on and caught her arm. "You could never look like an idiot. You're absolutely beautiful and much too adorable."

The tension in her body disappeared and her mouth parted in surprise. She pressed her hand against her forehead and shook her head.

"I'm sorry. I have absolutely no right to be jealous. I have no claim on you."

But she did. There was no way he could admit that right now. Until Nate and Christy were officially broken up, it just wouldn't be right.

He still had her arm, and used it to pull her body close to his. "If it makes you feel any better. Seeing you with Bubba made my blood pressure go up a few notches."

"It did?" Her eyes went wide, but her smile was smug.

"Sure did." He tucked a loose strand of her hair behind her ear.

Christy could be innocent at times, he decided, but this wasn't one of them. She'd known exactly what she was doing when she'd danced with Bubba. What she'd been hoping to achieve.

"What do you say we head back to my place?"

"Yes, please." She gave a wan smile. "I got up way too early this morning. I'm exhausted."

She did look tired, but still, he couldn't help riling her a little. "That nap didn't help today?"

He gave her a quick look as they walked out of the barn, his hand resting low on her back.

She laughed and fiddled with the same strand of hair he'd just tucked away. "So you did know what I was doing?"

He scowled. "Know? Hell, it was all I could do not to bust through the door and give you a hand."

"You should have done it then, because I'm too tired to even think about getting kinky right now."

"I could always change your mind." Adam tossed his hat into the back seat of his truck.

"Not tonight, cowboy." She yawned. "Not tonight."

Adam hid a smile as he started up the truck. If he wanted her, he could have her. But she'd need her sleep for tomorrow.

"How are you at riding?"

Christy glanced at him suspiciously. "I don't know. What kind of riding are we talking about? And I'm not trying to be all sexual with that question."

He gave a soft laugh. "Horses, darlin'."

"Ah." She shrugged and laid her head on his shoulder. "I haven't ridden a horse since girl scout camp back when I was eleven. But I was pretty good back then."

He liked having her snuggled up to him like this. It brought out the protective side in him. "Good. Tomorrow I'll put you on

Sadie and we'll go for a ride."

"Is Sadie the gentle horse?"

"Now why would I give you the easy horse?" He smiled and shook his head. "I know you like to be challenged, Christy. Sadie still needs to be broken in—I figure you can handle the job."

"*What?*"

"Just kidding, darlin'. Sadie's as easy as..."

"Mandy Lou?" Christy inserted, not sounding at all innocent.

Adam laughed again. Maybe it wasn't right, but it was kind of fun having Christy be jealous of Mandy Lou.

"I wasn't trying to be funny. Anyway, so what time are we riding in the morning?"

"Eight."

"Eight? Oh, come on that's a little early. Can't I sleep in?"

"Well, originally I was going to have us leave at five and catch the sunrise."

"Eight sounds perfect. I'll set my alarm. Or yours. Do you have one?"

"I'll wake you up."

Hmm. And he knew just the way he'd be tempted to do it. Crawl into bed with her and start by kissing her neck. Then he'd suck on her tight little nipples, while getting her nice and wet by rubbing her clit until she begged him.

Yeah, that'd be a nice little awakening for both of them. But it wouldn't get them on the trail on time. Not to mention it would prove his inability to stay away from her. It wasn't that he wanted to stay away, so to speak—he just needed to know he could. And he still had to make that phone call to Nate. Yeah. Tomorrow. He'd do it tomorrow.

She yawned again, and by the time they reached his house she was already half asleep. He almost nudged her awake and then thought better of it.

He unbuckled her seatbelt, and then got out of the truck to open her door. Slipping his hand under her thighs and behind her back, he scooped her up, kicked the door closed and headed inside.

She didn't wake, but did emit a soft little moan and turn her face into his chest.

Adam's chest swelled as he drew in a quick breath, his arms tightened around her protectively.

He carried her upstairs and set her down on the bed. Which only made him think about what she'd been doing on that bed earlier today.

Blood flooded to his cock and he bit back a groan. It was so tempting to just nudge her awake and—*No.*

He went to work pulling off her boots and smiled. Was this what she considered cowboy boots? What were they even made of? That sure wasn't leather.

She moaned and he lifted his gaze to her face. She was still asleep, looking so sweet and vulnerable. Christy, vulnerable? He almost laughed and just shook his head instead.

He hesitated before reaching for the zipper on her skirt. Tugging on the metal, he pulled it down and until he was able to slide the skirt off her.

She'd be okay in her T-shirt and panties, she'd certainly been earlier today. Before he could let that thought take hold and drive him nuts, he tucked a sheet around her.

"Mmm." She moaned again and rolled over onto her side.

Adam kissed her forehead, and then walked quietly out of the room.

Tap. Tap. Christy opened her eyes and stared at the wispy canopy over her head. Had someone been knocking on her door?

Tap. Tap.

"Christy?"

She groaned, rolled over and buried her face in the pillow. Surely it couldn't be morning already?

"Are you awake?" Adam called from the other side of her door.

"I am now. Is it really eight?"

"No. It's seven-thirty. We leave at eight."

Christy sat up and slid her legs off the bed. "Do I have time for a shower?"

"Can you shower, dress, and eat in a half an hour?"

"Of course." She opened the door and swallowed hard. God, he looked sexy for it being so early in the morning. His hair still wet from a shower, his jeans hugged him in all the right places. "Uh...do you have towels in the bathroom?"

"Sure do."

She lowered her gaze and swept past him. "Okay. I'll be ready at eight."

And she was. At eight o'clock exactly she was dressed in jeans, a tank top, and a pair of old running shoes. Breakfast was an apple that she still carried with her as they went out back to the stables. The scent of hay, horse, and manure permeated the air in the old wooden building.

"I'm impressed." He glanced at her as they walked past the first few stalls.

"Don't be, I can get ready in half that time if I need to. Now, which horse is mine?"

Adam swung open the gate to the stall they'd stopped in front of. The horse inside glanced up for a second, before it returned to munching on the hay.

"Here's your girl. Meet Sadie."

Christy stepped past him into the stall and gently stroked a hand down the horse's sleek brown back.

"She's pretty." *Just don't toss me the minute I climb up on you.*

"Do you remember how to saddle a horse?"

Christy tore her gaze away from Sadie long enough to give Adam an incredulous look.

"I was eleven when I learned, and I don't think I even paid attention then to how it was done. All I cared about was the fact that I was getting to ride a horse."

"Well, pay attention this time." Adam took Sadie by the halter, and led her out of the stables. He tied her to a post and said, "Today you're going to learn and retain the knowledge."

"Ah. Who's the teacher now?"

"I am, and don't you forget it, darlin'." He pulled all the equipment they needed out of the stable. "Hold on a minute while I grab Smokey."

Christy watched him go back into the stables. God he was sexy. It was those jeans, they just completed the whole cowboy image. He returned a moment later with a gray horse that was quite a bit bigger than hers.

"I've only been here a day, Adam, and it's been great. I'm really getting the whole country experience."

"Not everyone in Peppertown rides horses and two-steps. We have a lot of folks in town who go to the city just to see the opera and symphony. And the Langston boys couldn't give a damn about horseback riding—they got their motorcycles."

Christy giggled. *Ah, small towns. You had to love them.*

"Now, watch how I do this." Adam grabbed some kind of blanket type of thing. "This here is your saddle pad. Put it across the horse's back, just below his withers."

Christy grabbed the saddle pad, an Indian-style blanket that he handed her and did as he instructed on Sadie.

"Good. I'll put the saddle on for you, it's a little heavier. Did you ride English or Western at that camp you went to?"

"I don't know, how can I tell?"

"Did you have this here horn on your saddle before?" He gestured to the handle type thing at the front of the saddle.

"Yeah, it did."

"Good, then you should do just fine."

He swung the leather saddle up with ease. Christy groaned at the sight of his muscles flexing under his black T-shirt.

"Now you're going to tie the cinch around Sadie's belly. I'll do it this time, but watch how I do it. See how I tie it just behind her front legs?"

Did she ever. The way he leaned over, the jeans pulled tight over his muscular thighs and ass. Heavy pressure settled between her thighs and her nipples hardened.

"Christy?"

"What? Yes. Uh, yes I see." She groaned. *This isn't foreplay, you're saddling a horse for God's sake.*

Adam turned back to finish saddling his horse. "All right, you're all set. You wanna try to hop up on Sadie?"

"I'll sure try." She turned back to her horse. "Now the moment of truth. Can I actually get my butt up and in that saddle?"

"I'm going to love to see you try, darlin'."

Christy giggled as she grabbed the horn on the saddle. She slipped her left foot into the stirrup, and hopped up, but missed. She struggled a few times, but couldn't quite get all the way up.

Adam's hands circled her waist and he lifted her easily into the saddle. The contact burned through her tank top as she gripped the horn to steady herself.

"Thank you." She smiled down at him. "Although that was kind of cheating, I suppose."

"There's only so much perfection a person needs to have, darlin'. Besides, it gave me a reason to touch you."

"Then you can help me into a saddle any time, cowboy." Christy watched as he easily mounted his own horse. *Ugh, to be tall.* He made it look so easy. Like he was in one of those old country western films.

"You remember how to guide the horse, right?"

"I remember everything from this point on." She stroked Sadie's neck. "And since you've given me the gentle horse, I think we'll do just fine."

"All right then, just follow me." He turned his horse and started to lead her away from the house and onto a trail that led past the lake.

"Where are we going?" She had to yell after him, since she was a few feet behind.

"I have a nice little trail that goes through my property," he called back. "You can bring Sadie up next to me if you'd like. The trail's wide enough for a while."

Christy tapped her heels gently into the horse's sides and clicked her tongue, hoping the horse would pick up speed.

It worked. Sadie upped her pace, and a moment later their

horses were moving briskly down the trail side by side.

"This can't all be your property," she said in disbelief as she took in the acres of land and trees. They were still beside the lake, which looked pretty darn inviting in the heat. Sweat trailed down between her breasts and the back of her neck was already sticky.

"It sure is, and there's a whole lot more you'll get to see throughout our ride."

"God, what are you, some kind of millionaire? It must have cost a small fortune."

He didn't answer and she became more curious. Well, he was pretty successful. In fact, just last night his mom had mentioned how Adam's Apples was become one of the city's biggest employers. It wouldn't surprise her if he was über-rich, or not far from it.

She shifted in her saddle. Hmm. The thought made her a little uncomfortable the more she thought about it. So, not only was she in love with a cowboy, but a rich one.

Oh, God. Her breath caught. What was she thinking? In love with Adam? This fast? She shook her head. She wasn't the type to fall in love so easily. And certainly not with a man with a slow drawl and the kind of manners her grandma would have been proud of.

She didn't want to think about it right now. "Can we swim later?"

She gave the lake one more longing glance as they began to move away from it.

"Sure can. Are you wearing a swimsuit under those jeans?" His glance over at her told her just how much he appreciated the fit of her pants.

Christy's pulse jumped at his appraising look. "Do I need

one? The lake's on your property. Unless you have some objection to me swimming around naked in your backyard."

"Darlin', I never have an objection to you being naked. We can take a dip after our ride."

"Fantastic." She could already feel the cool water on her parched skin.

Adam gave her a curious glance. "My brother uses that word a lot."

"Does he?" She averted her gaze. That's right; it was one of Nate's favorite expressions. Did Adam find that weird at all?

"Yeah, he does. Has he called you since you arrived here?"

"No." Why was he asking? Hadn't she just told him they were taking time apart? "I don't mind. Besides, I'm sure he's busy."

And he probably was. Busy with Brian, the new boyfriend. Not that he was supposed to call her anyway. They hadn't made any plans for the exchange of phone calls. This was supposed to be her time alone with Adam.

Although, it probably would have been considerate of Nate to make sure she'd made it over the pass all right. But then somehow the word "consideration" had ceased to exist in Nate's vocabulary these past couple of weeks.

"We're heading up a bit of an incline," Adam told her. "And the trail's gonna get a little more narrow. So why don't you urge Sadie to fall behind Smokey and me."

"Will do." She pulled back on Sadie's reins and let Adam take the lead.

"You seem to be holding your own on a horse."

"Thanks, I'd forgotten how fun it is to ride." Christy shifted in the saddle. Hmm. Just how sore was she going to be at the end of the day, though?

"This here is part of the apple orchard." He gestured to the trees off to their right.

"Oh, let's pick one."

"They aren't ripe yet. They'll be ready come fall."

Christy sighed. "I guess I'll just have to come back when they're ripe."

Adam glanced at her over his shoulder and gave her a lopsided grin. "What makes you think I'm going to let you leave at all?"

Christy couldn't come up with a flippant reply to save her life. She was too thrown by the remark and the images it evoked. Adam asking her to stay with him. Life in a small town. Living a slower pace of life. Could she ever do that? Make the switch from city chic to country chick?

She stared at Adam's back and it started to become clear. When it came to him, anything was possible. He'd turned her monotonous life on its head.

They rode in silence for about another half-hour, when Adam turned to glance back at her again.

"My parents are going water-skiing on Lake Peppertown tomorrow. They were wondering if we wanted to go."

His parents were going water-skiing? Was he kidding? She frowned. "Water-skiing? Isn't that kind of dangerous?"

"Dangerous?" Adam glanced over his shoulder, giving her a look of disbelief. "How so?"

"I just wondered..." she hesitated, "...shouldn't your dad be taking it easy?"

"Why?"

"Well, he just had surgery."

"Oh, yeah, I forgot all about that." He shrugged. "Shouldn't be a problem."

"Really?" Her voice rose sharply. "I would think he would be on orders not to do anything too excitable after a bypass."

"Bypass? What are you talking about?"

Something in the back of Christy's head started tingling. She could have sworn Nate had said his dad had just gone through a bypass. "He...he didn't have a bypass? What kind of surgery did he have?"

"My dad had some hemorrhoids removed a few months ago, but that was the extent of it."

Christy paused. "I thought he had a bypass after his heart attack last year."

"Heart attack?" Adam stopped his horse and turned in his saddle so that he was looking at her. "Dad never had a heart attack. Where did you get such a crazy idea like that?"

Chapter Thirteen

She was going to kill him. Cut off Nate's balls, and then freaking kill him! Christy's vision blurred as Adam's words looped in her head. She ground her teeth together. Did she look as pissed as she felt? Damn, she was so close to blowing her lid right now.

Adam gave her a curious stare, but she tried her best to avert his gaze.

This time Nate had gone too far. This was completely, one-hundred percent inexcusable. The whole reason she'd agreed to go along with his charade had been lie. A freaking lie!

"Dad had an ulcer a while back," Adam said thoughtfully. "Maybe that's what you're thinking of."

"No."

"Hmm, then I don't know where you got such an idea."

She should just tell Adam everything, to hell with her promise. Just scream that Nate was gay and had been lying to everyone—her included. In fact, the moment she got back to the house she was going to call him and tell him the deal was off.

"Christy, you all right?" Adam asked, sliding off his horse and approaching her.

"Dandy." She kept her hard gaze focused on the trees beyond her shoulder.

"You sure don't sound dandy." He scratched the back of his neck and gave her a closer look. "Do you want to get down for a little bit and stretch your legs?"

"All right."

Easy, Christy, don't take out your frustration on Adam. If anything, he was the most innocent of the victims in this situation, besides his parents of course.

He clasped her waist and lifted her down from the horse. Adam's touch was like sunlight. All warm and tingly, and could get her hot if it lingered too long.

"Hey." His voice was soft and he kept his hands on her waist when her toes finally touched the ground. "What's going on?"

She laid her head against his chest and wrapped her arms around his waist.

"Nothing," she muttered into his cotton shirt. She took a deep breath and inhaled the smell of man, horse, and summertime. All her frustration just disappeared when he held her like this.

"Are you sure?" His hands smoothed up and down her back in a calming caress, and goose bumps broke out on her body despite the heat.

"Mm-hmm." She closed her eyes and nuzzled her cheek against his chest. "You feel really good. Hard and safe."

He laughed. "Careful what you're saying. You're not really safe when I'm hard."

"I wasn't talking about that," she chided, but now that he'd mentioned it, it definitely crossed her mind. And his too, apparently, because she could feel his erection pressing into her belly.

"I know you weren't." He pulled back and reached down to

take her hand. "Let's go have lunch."

"Lunch? It's kind of early. Did you really pack something?"

"It's almost eleven. I'm hungry, and I always come prepared."

Hmm. Did he bring along a condom, too? In case things got a little out of hand. Not like they were really going to have sex under an apple tree. That was taking the gravity theory a little too far.

Adam pulled a small sack and blanket out of the saddle bag, and walked under one of the trees that offered shade.

"Hot enough for you?" he asked, as she stumbled down to the blanket with a groan.

"I'm doing all right with the heat, but I can tell my thighs are going to hate me later."

"Saddle sore?"

"And then some."

His smile widened as he unwrapped some leftover fried chicken and biscuits.

"Wow. Did you bring wine, too?" she teased, and laughed as he proceeded to bring out two mini bottles of wine. "Oh, either you're trying to be romantic or you just got off a plane."

"I forgot glasses, so we're going to have to drink from the bottle. Are you okay with that?"

"Ah, just like college."

Christy took the mini bottle of chardonnay from him, amazed that it was still cold. He must've had them on ice in that bag.

Adam handed her a paper plate loaded with chicken and biscuits. She picked up a biscuit and nibbled on the buttery bread.

"Your mom is a fantastic cook." They'd settled at the top of the hill, and were up high enough that she could look out at his expansive property through the trees.

"Yes, that she is."

Christy twisted the cap off of her wine and took a small sip. He sure hadn't exaggerated about the size of his land. The house looked small from up here, and in reality it wasn't that big compared to some of the homes nowadays. But that's exactly how it should be, she thought. Just enough of a house to live in, and a whole lot of land to run around on.

When she thought about her apartment, it suddenly seemed more suffocating than before.

"So what do you think?"

She looked up at Adam's question. "About what? The food is fantastic and the view is amazing. Not to mention that your land leaves me speechless."

"I don't think I've ever seen you speechless, darlin'. You always have something to say."

Christy just smiled and finished the rest of her biscuit. It was a little frustrating. She had a lot to say, but half the time she wasn't allowed to say it.

As Christy turned again to look out at the view, Adam kept his own gaze on her wistful profile.

Boy she was a tough gal. She hadn't complained once about the stifling heat, or riding on a horse uphill for over an hour, which was an amazing feat for anyone. It was a blistering hot summer and the trail was dusty and uneven.

Actually, Christy was the first woman he'd ever taken up to this lookout. This was a special area for him. It was where he came to get away and regroup his senses. Get back to nature,

Tempting Adam

so to speak. And he'd wanted to share it with her, with Christy. To see the look on her face that he observed now.

He finished off the rest of his chicken, while continuing to study her thoughtfully.

"Why are you staring at me?"

Adam hid a smile. "Why not? You're beautiful."

"Please, so is this view." She turned to face him. "What's on your mind?"

"You. And how well you're adjusting to being over here."

"I've only been here a day," she protested, giving him an incredulous look. "I'm not going to freak out and run home in less than twenty-four hours."

"I'm glad to hear that."

And really, he had been a little worried. Some people got cabin fever in a small town, drove back out after a few hours. There weren't any big movie theaters, expensive restaurants, or air-conditioned shopping malls. No, Peppertown was just a sweet little small town. Where you went down to the diner for fresh lemonade and pie, and hit up the local mercantile for any kind of shopping you needed done.

Christy raised an eyebrow. "Tell me, cowboy. How does one make cider? Where would I begin, someone without big machines and stuff?"

Talk about a subject change. "Come on, you don't want to know that."

"I do. Tell me, I'm curious."

She was serious, he realized, and honestly seemed interested.

"Well. You need to use apples that aren't spoiled; in my cider we use different types." He paused to eat part of his biscuit. "Get the ripest ones, and then you've got to wash 'em, core 'em, and cut 'em."

"Then what do you do?" She reached out to wipe a bead of sweat off his forehead.

Her touch made him pause. Damn she looked sexy, adorably so with her damp skin and dust on her cheeks.

"Well, umm." He cleared his throat. *Cider, she's asking about cider.* "*We* use a fruit press since we produce large quantities at once. But say *you* were just going to make some at home."

"Yeah, what would I do? Without all the expensive equipment."

Adam's gaze followed Christy's hand as it trailed from her neck down to the low neckline of her tank top.

"You'd, uh...you'd want to chop up the apples in a blender, and then put them in a muslin sack. Squeeze them until the juice comes out."

"That's it? That's how you make cider? Hmm, sounds simple enough."

Her nipples were tight under the tank top she wore, Adam noticed them pushing against the thin cotton.

"No, that's just plain and simple apple juice. 'Course you have to pasteurize it first, but that's a different story." He slid forward, reaching out to trail his hand from the pulse in her neck to the valley between her breasts. "Speaking of heat, darlin', you're killing me here."

"Am I?" Her eyes narrowed, her mouth curving into a devious smile. She took another sip of wine and leaned back, her pert breasts rising towards him. "How do I turn the juice into cider?"

"It gets a little more complex there." He had to touch her. He covered her breasts with the palms of his hands and squeezed lightly.

She inhaled sharply. Her next words came out a bit unsteady. "I'm game. Go on."

He didn't miss the double meaning in her words, and reached for the straps of her tank top and bra, pushing them both off her shoulders and down to her waist.

"So, cowboy, what happens next?"

Christy's naked breasts were warm and soft under his hands, her nipples grazed against his palms. "You take the unpasteurized juice and let it ferment for a few days."

She gasped as he squeezed her flesh, kneading the shape of her. He laughed and drew his thumbs across the peaks of her breasts.

"Oh...go on."

"Okay, now's where it gets hard." He leaned forward and kissed the rapid pulse in her neck.

"Funny, I though it was already hard." She giggled, and sighed when he kissed the curve of her neck.

"Oh, it is." He winced, feeling his cock harden even more.

"So finish, Adam." Her nails caught on his back through his shirt.

"Finish?" he repeated and closed his mouth over one of the rigid nipples.

"Ooh...God...umm. Yes, cider. Oooh...how...?"

He dragged his tongue across the peak and was rewarded by her strangled cry. "Right. Cider. Well, after a few days the sediment will settle on the bottom and bubbles rise to the top. Then you need to do what's called racking off."

Christy lowered her hand between them and stroked his dick through his jeans. "Not to be confused with jacking off?"

He smiled and licked the other puckered nipple. "Do you want to hear this or not, darlin'?"

"Actually, no." She groaned and undid the fly on his jeans. "Can you just write it down for me later?"

"Hell, yeah." He popped the fly on her jeans and slowly dragged the tab down, then slipped his fingers into her panties to find her hot and wet.

He closed his eyes briefly, trying to keep control. "Damn, woman. All that talk about cider really turned you on."

"Yeah, something like that," she whispered raggedly.

Her slick cream coated his fingers, and he rubbed her swollen clit. Lord, she felt so good. How had he gone so long without touching her?

She groaned and lifted her hips against him, while freeing his cock from his jeans.

With the pressure off his dick and her hands now wrapped around it, it grew more difficult to think. Thank God she'd ditched the cider talk.

He applied more pressure to her clit and she gasped.

He lowered his head and bit one nipple, squeezing her clit lightly.

"Adam...*please*." Her eyelids started to flutter and he sank his fingers deep into her pussy.

She moaned and her hand tightened around his cock as she stroked it.

"Oh, Lord, Christy..." He groaned and thrust against her hand. "You're driving me crazy."

"Likewise." She pulled his jeans and briefs down and off his body.

He tugged her tank top and bra all the way off.

"I can't wait anymore." She jerked his shirt over his head.

"Nobody's asking you to." Grabbing the hem of her jeans, he dragged them off her legs and then ripped her panties from her body.

"Then let's do it." She grabbed the back of his head to pull his mouth down to hers.

Her words shredded his last bit of restraint—if he even had any—and he groaned, stroking his tongue against hers when she slid it into his mouth.

The sweet taste of wine, combined with her natural sweetness, muddled his mind. The kiss had never been innocent, but suddenly it got a whole lot wickeder.

Adam pressed her back onto the blanket so she lay beneath him, and deepened the kiss. Apparently she didn't like the position, and managed to roll them over so that he was on the bottom and she on top.

"Did you bring a condom, Adam?"

"Sure did." He reached out to his jeans and grabbed the condom out of the pocket, working quickly to sheathe his cock.

"Good boy." Christy scooted downwards so she was over his erection, and then began to lower herself onto him.

He watched her eyes close and her mouth part while feeling her hot sheath pulling his dick deeper. He tightened his grip on the curves of her ass, and thrust his hips upward, embedding himself to the hilt.

"Sweetness." He gasped and closed his eyes. "I've missed you, Christy."

"Oh, Adam..." She rotated on him, making the sexiest little groans. "God, me too."

Her pert breasts jiggled with each movement she made on top of him, and his gaze riveted on the puckered pink tips.

"Lean forward." He lifted his hands to her waist and urged her to lean down.

Christy obliged until her nipple brushed his lips. Adam opened his mouth and drew it inside, laving the sweet tip with his tongue. She moaned and her inner muscles clenched around him.

Adam curled his tongue over the tip, then closed his lips around her and sucked hard.

She whimpered and jerked on top of him, rocking back and forth.

He lifted his hips and thrust into her again, meeting her downward pushes. His grip tightened on her hips as he slammed up into her.

He released her nipple on a groan as she picked her own pace and rode him harder, faster.

"Christy!" His sac tightened with his approaching climax. Reaching between them, he found her swollen clit and squeezed.

She gasped and her inner muscles clenched around his dick.

"Oh God." He exploded with a groan and gripped her hips, staying buried inside her through the orgasm.

His legs trembled before he fell back against the grass. He traced his hands leisurely over the curves of her bottom. His heartbeat slowed as he continued to squeeze her ass.

"Mmm...that was fun." Christy drew her nails down his naked chest, and leaned down to brush her lips across his.

"I'd say," he just barely managed to mutter.

She nuzzled his neck. "But I think we should head back. I'm pretty sure my butt's sunburned now."

"You could be right." His caress turned into a light swat on her butt and she giggled. "Let's get going."

Christy climbed off him and grabbed her clothes, shimmying back into them. Damn she was sexy. Adam stood, jerked his gaze away and went to get himself dressed as well.

Once dressed, they collected their trash from lunch and folded up the blanket.

She glanced at him. "You know, I could really use some cooling off, for multiple reasons. Do you mind if we go swimming on the way back?"

"I think that sounds like a great idea. Let's head out."

A few minutes later they were on the horses again and riding down the hill. The ride back must have been harder for her, because every time he glanced behind him she was wincing.

They reached the lake and Adam started to dismount.

"No." Christy stopped him. "I can't swim. I won't even be able to walk when I get down. My thighs are killing me. Please, let's just go back to the house."

Adam laughed and grabbed the reins again, urging his horse the few hundred feet towards the stables. Once there, he quickly got off his horse and went to help her down from Sadie.

He lifted her from the saddle and set her down, catching her around the waist again when her knees buckled.

He frowned. She'd been serious about that sore bit. "You all right?"

"Fine." An obvious lie as she gave another miserable wince after taking a few steps. "What do we do with the horses now? Do we need to take off the saddle and brush them or something? All that post-ride stuff?"

"I'll take care of it," he told her, leading the horses back into their stalls. "Go on inside the house and get off your feet."

When she started to walk and it became more of a wide-legged swagger, he shut the door on the stall and went after her.

"Hold up, darlin'."

She stopped and turned to glance back at him, then gasped in surprise when he lifted her into his arms.

"I can walk," she protested. "You don't have to carry me."

"You look like a drunken gunslinger." He shifted her in his grasp. "Besides, I don't mind. Like I said, all the more reason to touch you."

She wrapped her arms around his neck and gave him a devious look. "You did plenty of touching up on the hill, Adam."

"You're right about that." Lord it felt nice holding her, with her bottom resting against his arm and his other hand brushing the underside of her breast. This was getting to be a habit. An addictive habit.

"I'm sorry about this." Christy gave him a pained smile. "I don't think a human's legs are supposed to spread that far."

"Sure they are. And I seem to recall you being in a similar position a couple of hours ago, only it wasn't on a horse," he teased and loved the way her cheeks went pink. "Besides, how do you think people got around before we had cars?"

"In a buggy *pulled* by horses."

He laughed and shook his head. "You're a rider, Christy. Admit it. I could see how much you loved being on Sadie. You just gotta give yourself a couple of days to break your body in."

She managed a small smile. "Actually, you're right. In fact, I want to go back out and ride tomorrow. Just maybe take the rest of the day off today."

Adam carried her into the house and then laid her down on the chaise lounge.

"I'm going to take care of the horses, just relax and I'll be back in a bit."

Chapter Fourteen

Adam walked back outside, hating to leave her but knowing the horses needed to be washed down and put away.

He rushed through the process so he could get back to Christy. When he came back inside, she was asleep right where he'd left her.

Ah, maybe he should just put her in bed. He lifted her up and started up the stairs. She stirred and opened her eyes.

"Ouch. I'm still sore." She tried to wriggle out of his grasp, but he had no intention of letting her go.

"Okay, you don't have to carry me upstairs for God's sake. This can't be easy."

"You're light enough. Besides, I did it last night, too," he reminded her. "I have a great idea."

"What's that? A prescription for muscle relaxers?"

He carried her into the bathroom. "No, even better. I'm going to draw you a bath."

He set her down and then went over to the claw-foot tub to turn on the faucet.

"Oh, you are a smart man, but then I already knew that." She pulled her T-shirt over her head.

Adam averted his gaze, but not before he saw the swell of her breasts covered by the blue satin bra. How the hell could he want her again so soon? He swallowed hard and stuck his hand under the water to check the temperature.

"I'd offer bubbles or something, but I don't have any of that kind of girly stuff."

"Do you have honey?"

"Honey?" He turned to her with a startled glance, then wished he hadn't when he saw that she had her jeans off and was about to peel off her panties.

"Yeah, it's a great moisturizer."

"Right. I'll go downstairs and grab some." But his body refused to move as he stared at the curves and shadows of her body now exposed to him.

"Honey, cowboy?" she reminded him, her tone light and her expression pure sin.

"Honey." He gave an abrupt nod and spun on his heel, hurrying back down the stairs. Her laughter followed him, then the sound of her climbing into the tub.

Adam grabbed the phone off the wall and dialed Nate's number. He needed to talk to him. Now. No more feeling guilty about this at all.

Nate's phone rang four times until it went to voicemail. Adam cursed, debated leaving a message and then just hung up. So much for that.

He grabbed the honey from the cupboard. It was local and fresh from the Wilsons' farm down the road.

He wasn't in such a hurry to get back upstairs. He knew she was waiting for him, naked in the tub. Too bad it wasn't big enough for both of them. Or maybe that was a good thing.

He walked back into the bathroom and groaned. Christy lay reclined in the tub, only partially submerged since it still hadn't filled completely. Her body arched against the curve of the tub, her nipples hard and pert in the air. She kept her eyes closed, but gave appreciative moans every few seconds.

"This is heaven." She didn't open her eyes. "Did you bring the honey?"

He blinked in surprise. "How did you know I was back?"

She opened her eyes and gave him a slow smile. "I heard your footsteps."

Adam unscrewed the lid from the jar of honey and knelt down beside the tub. He tilted the jar so the honey poured under the water in a thick and steady stream.

He shook his head. "I don't get it. Aren't you going to be all sticky?"

"Nah, not if I only use a little bit." She leaned forward and pushed the jar back in its upright position so the honey stopped flowing. But still a ribbon trailed onto the curve of her belly.

"Oops." She glanced down. "Do you have a wash cloth?"

His gaze dropped to her stomach. Instead of opening a nearby drawer to retrieve a cloth, he reached into the tub and massaged the honey over her belly and then into the thin patch of curls below.

"Adam." Her voice cracked as he toyed with the soft curls. "We already had sex earlier, and I don't think my legs can take the muscle-clenching orgasms you're so good at."

"Now if that doesn't sound like an invitation, I don't know what is." He didn't take his gaze from the pink wet folds between her legs. Unable to stop himself, he moved his fingers lower. "Besides, you only came once up on the hill."

"I'm not going to get pissy over having one orgasm," she protested. "And it was a really good one, Adam."

"Let me give you another really good one."

Adam smiled when, despite her protests, she rewarded him

by parting her thighs a little further.

"I want to please you again. The way you pleased yourself yesterday."

"When you were watching me?" She gasped when he pushed a finger slowly into her.

"Yes." He added another finger, loving the hot dampness he found inside.

Christy clutched each side of the tub and leaned back, closing her eyes.

He brushed his thumb over her swollen clitoris, watching her stomach contract with her quick indrawn breath.

"How does that feel?"

"Pretty ah...amazing. Even better if you keep doing it."

Adam laughed and circled the hot flesh with his thumb again, feeling her response in the liquid heat that coated his fingers. His own cock throbbed to life, but he ignored everything but her body and her response to him.

"You are so wet, darlin'."

"You make me this way, Adam." She panted and her body arched into his touch. "I love it when you touch me."

"Do you?" Her words inflamed him further, sending a wave of possessiveness through him. He leaned over the tub and caught one of her rigid nipples between his teeth, using his tongue to soothe the erect tip; his fingers moved deeper, his thumb stroking faster.

"Oh, God..." Her body trembled and her thighs squeezed shut around his hand as she started to climax.

"Yeah. Just like that," he murmured against her breast. "Let it take you, Christy."

Her body shuddered one last time and then went limp in the tub.

"God that came on fast," she said weakly.

"Yeah, it did. You went off like dynamite. A sexy little firecracker," he teased and ran his tongue over her nipple again. "Lord, I just can't seem to keep my hands off you."

"I don't want you to."

"Nate might."

She flinched and looked suddenly miserable.

Adam's gut clenched and he closed his eyes. *Damn.* Adam cursed himself and jerked a hand through his hair.

Why had he done it? Why had he brought up his brother after such an intimate moment? Bitter regret clogged in his throat.

They'd been doing so well at avoiding the subject of her and Nate's relationship and then he'd had to throw it in her face right after he'd brought her pleasure.

"I think I'd like to be alone now." She folded her arms across her breasts and leaned away, her tone suddenly weary.

Adam swore under his breath as he stood up. God, if only he could take it back.

"Thank you for the bath and..." She hesitated and then looked down at the water. "Anyway, thank you."

"I'll be downstairs." *You're a total ass, Adam.* He sighed and backed out of the bathroom. "I'll see you in a bit."

Once he'd left the room, Christy dropped her head against the back of the tub, tears pricking at the back of her eyes. This was so out of hand. Adam would never give in to exploring what they had together until Nate was out of the picture.

She had to do something about it. She had to put his mind at ease and bring closure to Nate's charade. Because it was a big, ridiculous mess now. He obviously wasn't happy enough with the time apart excuse.

A fat tear rolled down her cheek and she brushed it away, grinding her teeth together.

She was done putting her life on hold for Nate. It was over. Finished. Terminado.

Restless now, Christy climbed out of the tub and wrapped a towel around her. She pulled the plug to drain the water from the tub, and then headed back to her room.

She didn't stop to get dressed, but went straight to where her phone sat charging in the corner. She picked it up and dialed Nate's number. He didn't answer, and soon the voicemail came on.

Christy scowled as his chipper voice told her to leave a message. He was avoiding her. Nate always answered his phone. To let a call go to voicemail was practically sacrilegious in his book. Especially when she called.

"All right," she began her message. "You are in so much trouble, bucko. You lied to me about your dad. That's right, I know everything. It was hemorrhoids, not a heart attack. You played up the sympathy card and made me agree to some bogus charade. Well, you know what? I'm done. It's over. Got it? I'm not going to pretend to be your undersexed girlfriend—"

The voicemail beeped, signaling her time had run out. She cursed and redialed his number, waiting for the message to come on again.

"Oh, I'm not through with you," she went on. "Listen, Nate. I like your brother. I like him a lot. And maybe you think he's some egotistical player, but I think he's changed. Adam is incredible. Maybe if you took the time to talk to him you'd realize that."

She took a deep breath. "So, yeah. Call me."

She shut the phone and chewed on her lip in frustration. What was she going to do now? She could go downstairs and tell Adam she'd just broken up with Nate, but it would probably be better if she waited for Nate to call her back. So they could get their stories straight.

Relief that this would finally all be over made her body weak.

Nate might have been acting like a total jerk for the past few days, but guilt would win out. Deep down he was a good person. She knew this. It was just lately that he'd gone off his rocker. He just had to get his act together again.

Christy threw on her clothes and then went downstairs to talk to Adam. She found him in the kitchen reading the local paper. Hearing her approach, he glanced up when she walked in, his gaze conveying his regret.

"You didn't stay in there very long."

"The water got cold fast," she lied, not wanting him to feel responsible for her short-lived bath. She sat down at the table across from him.

"I'm sorry, Christy. I shouldn't have brought Nate up."

She shrugged. God, what she wouldn't give to tell him right now. "It's okay. So, got any big plans for the rest of the day?"

"I have a meeting with some of my employees in an hour. We have a lot to discuss with the fall harvest just around the corner." He glanced at her. "Do you want me to drop you at my parents' house? I don't want you to be bored, and I'm sure they'd love to see you."

"I think I'll stay here," she replied. "Do you mind if I hop on your computer and check my email?"

Adam stood up, coming around to tug gently on a strand of her hair.

"Can't let that stuff go, can you? Little Miss City girl," he murmured. "Help yourself. My password to get on the Internet is taped to the monitor."

Christy laughed in amusement. "Of course it is, because you're such a trusting country boy. You'll be back soon?"

"A couple of hours. Don't have too much fun while I'm gone."

He left without kissing her, and disappointment clawed at her stomach. But maybe things just needed to slow down.

If she put herself in his mindset, she could see why he'd be a little more hesitant. He was probably still hung up on the fact that they'd had sex again.

Standing up, she went and checked her email. She did her usual scan and decided on the level of importance, before responding to her mother's first.

Once that email was sent off and her mother's usual prattling worries taken care of, she logged off the Internet. After all the windows were closed and she was staring at the desktop, she noticed a file labeled "Adam's pics".

Curious, Christy double-clicked on it. Was she being too nosy? Ah hell, did it matter? She was going to look anyway.

The file popped up, displaying nearly a hundred thumbnail pictures of random people and places. She could easily spot Adam in some, and when she saw one with Nate she opened it up to the full size.

It was a picture of Nate and Adam a couple of years ago. She knew the date because Nate was wearing all black, and she remembered when that phase had started and ended. He'd been obsessed with avoiding all colors. She'd always thought it was kind of morbid and was glad when he'd decided to explore neutral tones.

The picture was of the brothers sitting at a picnic table. Adam looked relaxed with an easy smile on his face, but Nate's smile seemed brittle and he didn't look comfortable having his picture taken. That was a little unusual, because Nate was an attention whore and loved being photographed.

*Poor Nate...*he really was ill at ease around his family. It was so sad, she thought as she closed the photo and scanned the others. Her attention was snagged by a blur of red in one of the small photos. Suspicious, she honed the arrow from the mouse in on it and double-clicked.

Sure enough, a photo of Mandy Lou and Adam popped up. They must've been at some kind of Halloween party. She was dressed in a Playboy bunny costume and he as a gangster. She was sitting on Adam's lap, gazing down at him with lust in her eyes. Fortunately Adam was looking across the room and didn't seem to notice.

Great. Just great. Now she had to sit here and wonder exactly what kind of relationship Mandy Lou and Adam had had in the past. Or present for that matter.

"She looks ridiculous," Christy muttered bitterly, looking at the picture again.

Mandy's breasts were nearly popping out of the costume and she was showing more leg than a commercial for Nair.

Christy closed out the picture section. She'd rather not come across any more surprises like that one. She shouldn't have even looked in the first place.

Standing up, she stretched and glanced at the clock. Okay, that had taken a whole half-hour. Adam would probably be gone another few.

She went into the kitchen. Hmm. Maybe she'd try to whip up something for them to eat for dinner. Hopefully he wasn't the stereotypical bachelor with nothing but condiments in his fridge.

She opened the fridge. Not bad. The boy was stocked. Fruits, cheese, meats, vegetables—well, one vegetable, a bag of baby carrots. They had a lot in common food-choice wise. Then again, she'd figured that out after she'd cooked for him in her apartment.

She flipped on the kitchen radio and sighed as country music came on. Ah, well. It was starting to grow on her anyway.

An hour later she had a homemade tomato sauce simmering on the stove, garlic toast cooking in the oven, and was humming along to Kenny Chesney.

"Will you look at that." Adam's voice came from behind her as he walked into the kitchen. "I do believe I've died and gone to Italy."

Christy gasped and turned from the stove in surprise, managing to drop the wooden spoon into the sauce.

"You could have let me know you were here," she grumbled, reaching down to pick up the spoon and then going to rinse it off. "I thought I'd make some dinner."

"That's awfully sweet of you, darlin'. You didn't have to, though." He glanced at the stove. "Not that I'm complaining. That smells pretty darn good."

"Did you work up an appetite today?" she teased, thinking about the ride, the other kind of ride, and then the bathtub moment. "I figured you'd be a little hungry after our...busy day."

"You figured right." His gaze held hers and her pulse tripled at the heat there. He took off his hat and sat down at the table.

"It'll be ready soon." She turned back to the stove and checked to see if her noodles were boiling.

"Hey, some of the men at work want us to come have drinks with them tonight."

"Really?" She glanced over at him, excitement sparking inside her at the idea of going out. "That could be fun. We should totally go."

"It's a pretty wild bar." He shrugged. "Tuesday nights they have a bull-riding contest."

"Mechanical?"

"No, a real one," he drawled with light sarcasm. "Yeah, a mechanical one. You ever ridden a mechanical bull?"

"Can't say that I have. But I'm sure I'd be good at it." She drained the pasta and then dished them both up a plate, ladling the sauce on top.

"It's not as easy as it looks. Especially when you've been drinking, or depending on who's operating it."

She placed four giant meatballs on the pasta and then set the plate in front of him. "I'm game. I even have the perfect outfit to wear."

He gave her a skeptical glance that disappeared when he looked down at his food.

"This looks great." He picked up a fork that was on the table and dug in. "I kind of like having you here, Christy."

She sat down across from him, willing her pulse to slow back down. "I kind of like being here. The air's not as toxic."

He laughed. "Is that the only reason why?"

She smiled and gave him an innocent look. "Of course, should there be another reason?"

"I was hoping I might have something to do with it."

Christy took a bite of her own pasta and then leapt back up, having forgotten about the bread in the oven. She set a slice on his plate and then one on hers.

"You do." She glanced back up. "And that's why I broke up with Nate while you were gone."

Chapter Fifteen

Why had she said it now? The silence in the room made Christy question her spontaneous decision to tell him. Right after he'd flirted with her so adorably and she'd just prepared a nice spaghetti dinner.

"I just thought you should know," she said, keeping her tone even. "So if you'd like to go upstairs and have kinky-ass sex with me, you don't have to feel bad about it."

The silence on his end was uninterrupted and the tension in her body increased.

She cleared her throat, which felt suddenly tight. "I thought that would be good news to you, but maybe I was wrong."

"How did he take it?"

She'd told him in a message, so it wasn't like he could reply. Not like he'd be upset. They weren't even a couple.

"He, uh, didn't say much."

"Well, hell." Adam set down his fork and stared at his plate. "I don't know what to say. It just doesn't feel right."

Didn't feel right? How could it not feel right? Disbelief slammed into her, a flush of hot anger worked itself up through her body. "Let me get this straight. You don't want me anymore now that I'm available?"

"That's not what I said," he muttered and looked down.

"Uh, you didn't have to, cowboy. It was written all over your face." She stood up. The thought of eating food made her sick now.

"Come on, Christy. Sit down and finish your dinner. We just need time to sort things out."

"No, you need time to figure things out. I need a drink. Maybe I'll walk to the bar." The anger inside was just getting worse. *Didn't feel right? After he'd just slept with her that afternoon?* "Who knows, maybe Bubba will be there. I'm sure he'll still want me."

"You don't want Bubba." His eyebrows drew together and he scowled. "We both know you don't want Bubba."

Christy made a face at him. God, she just wanted to dump the plate of spaghetti on his head. Of course she didn't want Bubba. She didn't even know why she'd said that. Probably to upset him just as much as he'd upset her.

Why had she thought things would just be all right once Adam thought she was single? Apparently things couldn't get better, they could only get worse.

Without another word to Adam, she left the kitchen and walked upstairs. She paced her room, her blood boiled and frustration ate away at her. Where did they go from here? What was next? If there *was* anything to be done next.

Adam either wanted to be with her or he didn't. It really shouldn't have been that hard of a call.

"Could this suck anymore?" Christy groaned and looked down at her suitcase.

She went over and unzipped it, searching through it for her special outfit. The one she'd packed that was pure country—well, her version of pure country—and would give every man in the room a hard-on. And she'd bought it all at a thrift shop on Broadway.

Well, besides the hat and boots. They'd still been bought on Broadway, but were brand new and cost a heck of a lot more money.

She would go to that bar tonight, and she would look hot. It shouldn't take Adam too long to figure out what he'd be giving up.

She pulled on her panties first and glanced in the full-length mirror. Hmm. Well, maybe the panties weren't completely country, but they were certainly cute and girly. And besides, who would be seeing them besides Adam? And even that wasn't a guarantee.

"Dumb ass," she muttered under her breath.

She reached for the skirt next. It was knee-length, white cotton, with images of cowboy boots all over it. The shirt she pulled on was what really made the outfit sexy. It was a brown crocheted tank top that was low cut and ended high. She hesitated after reaching for a bra. Hmm. The bra straps would show if she did the bra.

One of the perks of having smaller breasts was the ability to skip the bra every once in awhile. She tossed the bra back into her suitcase. Screw it. The stitching on the top was small.

Only in bright lighting and up close would somebody almost be able to see her nipples through the top. It was the "almost" part that made the top so sexy.

Her cell phone came to life and she hurried over to grab it. *Please let it be Nate.* She glanced down at the caller ID. It was!

"Hi," she answered, flipping it open. "You got my message?"

"He left me, Christy!" Nate wailed into the phone.

"Who left you?"

She walked over to the mirror. Might as well get the makeup done while he unloaded.

"Brian. He left me for a waiter at Denny's."

Christy paused in the act of putting on bronzer. "Now wait. Brian, the drama major you were dating?"

"Uh, yeah." His tone turned snarky and she could hear him blow his nose into a tissue. "I'm so much better than a waiter at Denny's, aren't I?"

"Of course you are, Nate. You're way better. Jeez, that really sucks. I'm sorry, hon. I know you thought it would be different with him."

"I did. I really did!" He groaned. "What did I do to deserve this?"

"Nothing. Cheating men just happen. It's a fact of life. Get used to it." Christy hesitated, not really wanting to bring up her earlier phone call, but knowing she had to. "Look, you got my message, right?"

He sniffed. "Yeah, I got it. We're broken up. Fine. Whatever. I'm tired of the charade too."

"Oh, good. You have no idea what a relief this is." She went back to putting on makeup. "I don't know how much longer I could have kept this up. Your parents are really starting to like me and I feel bad deceiving them."

She didn't add that she was half in love with Adam, too. Although Nate probably had figured it out.

"I knew they would." He blew his nose again. "Look, I'm going to let you go now. I need to make myself an appletini."

"Maybe you should avoid drinking right now, Nate. It's just going to make you more depressed."

There was a harsh knock on her door and Christy shot it a worried glance. *Shit! Had Adam overheard any of her conversation?*

"Look, I've got to go. I'll call you later." She closed her

phone.

"What do you want?" She smoothed her skirt down.

"To talk."

"So talk then."

She reached for her calf-high, brown leather boots with three-inch heels and zipped them up.

"Did you want to skip the bar?" Adam asked through the door. "We could go down to the grocery store and pick up a DVD instead."

A DVD? Christy rolled her eyes and grabbed her cowboy hat off the dresser. She placed it on her head, leaving the hair under it to hang straight around her shoulders.

After another glance in the mirror, she went to the door and swung it open. "I'm going to a bar tonight, Adam. You're welcome to come with me or I could take a cab."

He stared at her and his jaw dropped, he snapped it shut again so loud that she heard it click. But she hadn't missed the raw desire in his eyes before they'd become censuring.

"Peppertown doesn't have cabs." His gaze continued to move over her body. "You're wearing that?"

"Sure am. Is there a problem?"

His jaw-line went even more rigid. "No problem."

"Good. I wanted to try to look a little more country tonight."

"You think that's what country gals look like?" He relaxed a bit as his mouth curved into a smile.

"I don't know." She shrugged and placed a hand on her hip. "But I have a theme going on, so work with me here."

He stepped into the light of the room and his gaze suddenly honed in on her breasts.

"I can see your—"

"No, you can't. You just think you can," she interrupted calmly.

"I'm pretty sure I can, Christy."

"You already know what they look like, so you're filling in the blanks."

Adam looked away and cursed, thrusting a hand through his hair. "What about those jeans you wore this morning? Those looked really nice on you."

"I'm wearing this."

"All right." He sighed, didn't look pleased, but gave in. "You ready to go?"

"One more thing." She turned back to her suitcase and pulled out a bottle of her favorite perfume, then spritzed a dose in-between her breasts. "Okay, we can go."

Adam cursed himself all the way to the bar. With Christy-the-sex-kitten sitting next to him, he had a rock-hard erection. Her perfume tickled his nostrils, and the fact that he knew exactly where it came from made him even crazier.

And every man at the bar was going to have the same damn reaction. His jaw tightened and his blood pressure jumped another notch.

"Is Candy Lou going to be there tonight?"

"Mandy Lou," he corrected her, even though he knew she'd been deliberate in her mistake. "And yes, she probably will be there."

"Oh, wonderful." Christy gave him a saccharine smile. "I do hope we can be friends."

"Did you get into my liquor cabinet before we left?"

Christy laughed and shook her head. "I didn't know that you had one. You should have mentioned it earlier. I would've loved to get a pre-buzz going."

Adam winced. So she was planning on getting loaded? He'd never seen her drink heavily since they'd met. Why was tonight so different?

They reached the bar and Christy climbed out of the truck, striding inside without him. What the hell had gotten into her?

And then he figured it out. She was pissed. Completely and one-hundred-percent pissed off at him. Hmm. Was it because he hadn't jumped up from the table with excitement when she'd just told him she'd dumped his brother? Could she really expect that from him?

Yeah, he wanted her. More than he'd ever wanted a woman before. But now that he could actually be with her, he felt a little guilty about it. And maybe that was a crappy way to feel, but he did.

Like when they'd been growing up and Adam would steal one of Nate's toys. Only this time it had been Nate's woman instead of a Transformer.

And then he'd overheard Christy telling Nate not to drink because it would make him more depressed. Well, hell. That pretty much made him feel like he deserved the asshole of the year award.

He needed time to think about this, maybe talk to Nate and clear the air. Yeah, there was an idea. He'd give Nate a call. But first things first. He needed to make sure Christy wasn't getting in over her head.

He strode into the dim bar and was met by the sound of a Gretchen Wilson song. He had to search for a moment before he saw Christy standing at the counter talking intently to Frank the bartender. She shook her head and started gesturing with her hands.

Adam sighed and went over to her. "What's she asking for,

Frank?"

Christy gave him a haughty glance and turned back to the middle-aged man.

"I just said I'd prefer an imported beer."

"We ain't got no imported beer, Adam." Frank rolled his shoulders and gave him a despondent look. "I keep telling her, but she insists I'm lying."

"Christy?" Adam gave her a quizzical look. Lord, she must be beyond pissed if she was picking a fight with a soft-hearted man like Frank.

Guilt flashed in her gaze and she muttered, "Fine, I'll take a Bud Light."

Frank nodded and poured her a glass of beer, then slid it across the counter towards her.

When she had the beer in hand, Christy turned to look around at the people in the bar.

Adam had already noticed one or two men checking her out. A moment later his friend Jason wandered over, his eyes glued to Christy.

"Hey there, Adam." Jason didn't even bother to look at him. "Who's this pretty gal?"

"Christy Wallace, and you are?" She stuck out her hand before Adam could even think about making the introduction himself.

"Jason Nielson," he replied and swallowed hard, taking her hand and pumping it eagerly.

Adam resisted the urge to smack the younger man upside the head. Jason was one of his employees, who he also considered a friend. He was a good ten years younger than Adam and still innocent enough to be struck dumb by a good-looking woman.

"Hmm. Well, nice to meet you, Jason. I take it you're a friend of Adam's?"

"Yeah, and I also work for him." He swallowed hard and looked back and forth between them. "Are you one of Adam's...friends?"

Christy gave Adam a sideways glance. "I'm not really sure what I am to Adam. But the night's still young. If you'll excuse me, I'm going to mingle."

Adam watched her walk away. Her petite body swaying in all the right places.

"Damn, Adam." Jason shook his head, his gaze also on Christy's ass. "I wouldn't mind getting myself a girl like that. But what's with her skirt?"

"She thinks its how we dress in the country." Adam's mouth relaxed into a grin. "She's from Seattle."

"I figured she wasn't local. Well, keep that one in your sight. She looks like trouble." Jason tapped his beer bottle against Adam's. "I'll see you later, boss."

You have no idea how much trouble that girl is. But I do. When he saw Christy talking to some women near the bar, he figured it would be a good time to call Nate.

He stepped outside the bar again and dialed Nate on his cell phone. It went straight to voicemail, so he left a message for his brother to call him back.

Adam shoved his phone into his back pocket and was about to stride into the bar, when he saw Mandy Lou leaning against the wall, smoking a cigarette.

"Hey, there," she murmured. "Didn't you promise to buy me a drink a few weeks ago?"

More like a few months ago.

"Because I could really go for a beer, and I seem to have left my wallet at home."

There was a bar full of men who would trip over themselves to buy Mandy a beer. He should just open his mouth and tell her that, because the last thing he needed was for Christy to get any more pissed off. But hell, she was already pissed at him anyway.

"One beer, Adam." Mandy Lou gave a throaty laugh. "Really, it's not like I'm asking you for a ring."

"Sure," he answered with a tight smile. "I'll buy your beer."

Her smile turned smug as she slipped an arm around his waist.

"Good boy. I figured you would."

Ah shit, Christy was really gonna flip her lid now. Adam took a deep breath as they walked through the doors together.

Chapter Sixteen

Where in the hell had Adam gone? Christy gnawed on her lip and scanned the bar again. She'd been looking for ten minutes and hadn't seen any sign of him.

That's what you get, Christy. You shouldn't have tried so hard to push his buttons all night. She swallowed a sigh. Maybe she had gone too far with the beer hissy fit. What if he'd actually left her here to find her own way home? No, Adam was way too much of a gentleman to do that.

The tension in her shoulders eased as she spotted him coming in the front door. But then she spotted Mandy Lou wrapped around his arm, and her blood pressure shot up again. The jerk! Oh God, she was going to lose it.

What the hell was he trying to pull? Her mouth tightened into a grim line as she tried to ignore the stab of hurt and jealousy.

She turned back to the bartender and ordered another beer, downing half of it before locking her gaze back on Adam and Mandy Lou.

"I don't get it." Suddenly Jason stood next to her again. "I thought he was with you?"

"Yeah, me too," she muttered and tilted the bottle back, taking out another quarter of her beer.

"Hot damn. I don't think I've ever seen a woman drink a beer so fast. You're nearly done with that one and you just ordered it. Would you allow me to buy you another?"

"I don't think..." She stopped and looked at Adam again. *Ah, hell, at this rate maybe getting sloshed was probably the best choice.* "Thank you, Jason. That's sweet of you. I'd appreciate that very much."

Jason's smile doubled in brightness, and he gave a quick goofy nod before hurrying off to grab her beer. Christy glanced away and saw Adam approaching with Mandy Lou in tow.

"Hey there, Christy. You remember Mandy, right?" he asked once they had come to a stop in front of her.

To be nice or not to be nice. Ah, hell, her mood was already on the downswing. "How could I forget hair that big?"

Mandy Lou's smug look vanished and her eyes narrowed. "That's quite a skirt you're wearing, Christy. Did you pick that up at a thrift shop?"

"Actually, I did. Isn't it great? I figured that since I'm in the country, I should try to act the part."

Mandy Lou tilted back her head and let out a musical laugh that had Christy's teeth snapping together. "Oh, honey, nobody around here dresses like that."

"Maybe you should. You might have better luck with the men." Christy turned a flirtatious smile up at Jason who'd just arrived back with her beer.

Out of the corner of her eye, she noticed how Adam's gaze hardened when he looked at Jason. How stupid. He'd obviously been the one to throw this mix of people together and now he was going to get jealous?

"You promised to buy me a beer, Adam." Mandy Lou turned her annoyed glance up to him. "Why don't you go get that for me while I tell Charlie to turn on the bull."

Adam was going to buy Mandy a beer? Oh, this was war. *Focus on the positive, girl.*

"Oh, that's right." Christy swallowed down her anger with another sip of beer and turned her gaze to the mechanical bull. "I get to ride a bull tonight."

"They won't let you ride if you're drunk." Adam's tone was laced with disapproval.

"I'm not drunk. Nowhere near it," she lied, meeting his hard gaze.

In truth, after this beer Jason had just brought her she'd be pretty buzzed. Being a total lightweight had its advantages and disadvantages.

Adam gave her a look that clearly said he didn't agree, then turned and walked to the bar.

Her stomach dropped and she looked away from his retreating back. This was just ludicrous. Why would he sit there and flirt with Mandy Lou?

Even if he *had* decided that he wanted to discontinue his relationship with her, he didn't have to flirt with another woman right under her nose. It was just mean. And he could've at least said something.

The idea that he might be doing just that made her nauseous. She took another drink of beer.

This must be how Nate had felt earlier. Only Mandy Lou didn't work at Denny's. Denny's sounded like an upgrade from Mandy Lou.

She scowled and downed the rest of her beer, setting the bottle on the table. When she looked up, Mandy had climbed onto the bull.

She started up, her body gyrating and writhing. All the men

hollered and made suggestive comments, and Mandy Lou positively preened from the attention.

"That doesn't look so hard," Christy grumbled. "I bet I could kick her ass at bull riding."

"It's harder than it looks." Jason gave her a worried glance. "Are you really thinking of trying it?"

"Sure am." She kept her gaze on Mandy Lou who still bucked on the bull.

It was pretty sexy-looking, she decided. Mandy Lou stayed on the bull until the operator slowed it, and she swung each long, denim-covered leg off.

"My turn." Christy stood, a bit unsteady on her feet and turned to walk over to the bull. Oh God, she was indeed buzzed. She hesitated for about two seconds. Maybe this wasn't the best idea.

Ah screw it. Of course it was. She'd show Adam—and every other man there—just how sexy she could be bouncing on a piece of metal.

She lifted her head and strode towards the center of the ring.

Adam shook his head when he saw Christy striding purposefully towards the bull. Damn, she better know what she was doing.

Jason approached him from the side and sat down in an empty chair. "Do you mind if I ask what's going on with you and that pretty lady?"

"Yes, I do," Adam answered, not even trying to be polite.

"I just think it was a little harsh the way you were flirting with Mandy Lou," Jason said hesitantly. "Christy seemed a little upset."

"I wasn't flirting with Mandy, she just called me on a beer I owed her. And Christy's a big girl, she can handle herself."

"Hell, I know that." Jason scowled. "She held her own with Mandy Lou, which isn't for the tender-hearted."

"Trust me. You were right when you said she was trouble. The girl can't seem to stay out of it."

Adam left him and went to the roped-off area where the bull riding took place.

He arrived just in time to see Christy getting helped onto the bull by one of the local men. The man's hand lingered on her butt a little longer than necessary, and Adam's eyes narrowed and his stomach burned with jealousy.

Christy got seated and then winked down at the man, her lips moving in an inaudible thank you.

Adam's grip on the beer tightened and he barely noticed when Mandy Lou came to stand next to him again.

"Did you like the way I rode that bull?"

"What?" He didn't look away from Christy who was giggling and prompting the controller to start the bull.

"The bull. Did you like the way I rode it?" Mandy Lou repeated, her tone impatient now. "That little show was for you, Adam. Did you like it?"

"Sure."

Christy began to move back and forth as the bull started up. Damn, hopefully she could hold on. But then she had experience in a saddle from riding a horse, so maybe she'd be able to stay up for awhile.

"Thanks a lot."

Adam glanced away from Christy for a moment. Mandy Lou obviously hadn't liked his response, and walked away from him. Thank God. He didn't have time for Mandy's spoiled antics.

His gaze shot back to Christy. The operator of the bull slowly adjusted the speed to go faster, but still she held her own. And she looked damn sexy bouncing, arching, and gyrating up there.

Every man in the bar had his eyes glued to her petite body, which was riding the hell out of that mechanical bull.

Her cheeks were flushed. She looked excited and even aroused as she flowed with jerky movements. Every man in the bar was probably imagining what it would be like to have Christy ride him that way.

"Yee-haw!" she yelled and then laughed. "Cowgirl up!"

Adam's breathing grew more labored as he watched her, the crotch of his jeans started to feel a little too tight as his erection rubbed against it.

Out of the corner of his eye, he saw a flash of red at the control table. He glanced over just in time to see Mandy Lou take over the controls.

"Holy hell!" He broke into a full run to stop what he knew was about to happen. He was too far away. There was no way he could get to the controls in time.

Sure enough, Mandy Lou had turned the bull up to its full speed. Christy's scream of excitement turned to pure terror as she went flying off and over the bull. She landed flat on her stomach, with her skirt up around her waist.

Every man in the bar ran to help her—once they got over the sight of her pink panties with the ruffles on her ass.

"Back off. Everyone just back off."

Adam pushed the horde of men aside and helped Christy up, smoothing the skirt back down over the blatantly sexy sight.

"You okay, darlin'?" His gaze and hands ran over her body,

checking for cuts or anything that might have been broken.

"I'm great!" she cried in excitement, wobbling a little on her feet. She glanced back at the bull. "That was so much fun. Can I do it again?"

"I think that's a great idea." Mandy Lou smirked, coming up beside them.

Adam pushed Christy gently behind him and turned to give Mandy Lou a fierce glare.

"That was out of line, Mandy."

"Oh, jeez, Adam. You're no fun. Lighten up a little." Mandy Lou shrugged and walked off, obviously tired of trying to get his attention and moving on to someone who would appreciate her.

"Come on." He grabbed Christy's hand and tugged her out of the ring.

"Hey, I wanted to go again," Christy protested as he led her down a hallway, and then into the empty bathroom.

His blood pounding, the adrenaline and lust running through him made him irrational.

He locked the door and turned to face her. It was insane how much he wanted her. Even though he knew his brother was back in Seattle nursing a broken heart because she'd dumped him, Adam wanted her.

He looked down at her breasts, rising and falling under the pitiful excuse for a top. It was no bigger than one of his grandma's doilies and had just as many holes.

"Wow, what's gotten into you?" she asked breathlessly.

"You got that backwards, darlin'." He walked towards her, narrowing his eyes and giving her a predatory smile. "What's gotten into you? And the answer is me."

"What? Adam…" Christy broke off on a squeak as he backed her up against the sink and then lifted her onto the counter.

"Are you going to tell me you don't want this?"

He pulled the straps of her tank top down until her breasts were bared.

Her eyes widened and she licked her lips. "I...no, I definitely want this."

She groaned as he lowered his head and sucked one of her firm, pink nipples into his mouth.

"Oh..." She shoved her fingers into his hair, holding him against her breast. "I thought you might not want this."

He drew back, licking the tight tip of her breast and reveling in her moan.

"I do. God, I do." He molded her pert breasts in his hand and took her nipple between his lips again.

Her head fell back and bumped the mirror, and the movement just aided in pushing her breast further into his mouth. He sucked harder, his tongue rasping over the hard tip. Then he closed his teeth closed over it and tugged gently until she cried out again.

"Adam..." She moaned and then went quiet when he transferred his mouth to her other breast. "How do you do this to me? Make me want you so much."

He stood between her spread thighs and rubbed his palm over the satin of her frilly pink panties. Hot wetness met his palm and he groaned.

"I've got to taste you."

He pulled his mouth away from her breast and dropped to his knees, grasping the sides of her panties and pulling them down her legs and then off.

"Oh, God. Maybe we shouldn't be doing this here." She gasped, as he slid her legs over his shoulders. Her skirt covered his head like a tent. He ignored her protest and buried his face in the hot sweetness between her legs.

She moaned loudly and her thighs clenched around his head. The taste of her set him on fire and he thrust his tongue deeper into her wet pussy, stroking upwards to find her swollen clit.

Each of his hands cupped a round cheek of her ass, and he tightened his grasp, pulling her snug against his seeking mouth.

She screamed while he fucked her with his tongue. He didn't care one bit that anyone out in the hallway could hear her. He kept on swirling his tongue around the heart of her, and then pressed a finger inside her tight asshole.

Her groan was guttural and he felt her tart juices flowing faster on his tongue. Her body began to shake from the oncoming orgasm.

"Oh God!"

Adam stayed with her, breathing in her musky scent. Loving her taste as she came in his mouth. Her thighs and stomach trembled. Her moans continued until she was limp and breathing heavy.

Adam stood up, lowering her legs back down so they rested against the counter, and then stood up. He started to reach for the zipper on his jeans when there was a knock on the door.

"Hello? Is someone in there? I need to pee."

Christy's eyes went wide and she pressed a palm against her mouth. He could tell she was trying not to laugh as she slid off the counter and grabbed her panties, stuffing them into her purse.

"We'd better go," she whispered and pulled her top back up, drawing in an unsteady breath.

"Let's go home, darlin'."

He pulled her against him, kissing the curve of her ear. Then he opened the door to the bathroom and escorted them past a very shocked-looking Mandy Lou.

Chapter Seventeen

The whole drive home, Adam could think of nothing but burying his cock deep inside Christy. The taste of her desire for him was still sharp on his tongue.

You should just send her to her own bed. His conscience pricked to life again as they climbed out of the truck and headed for the house. *At least call Nate and resolve things before you sleep with Christy again. What the hell happened to your self-control?*

He shook his head, remembering the way they'd lost control at the bar. Well, more so him. Dragging her into the bathroom and going down on her. Lord, the lengths she drove him to. The way she made him just lose it.

He opened the door to the house and Christy turned to him with questioning eyes. Almost as if she knew he hesitated to make love to her.

She held out her hand, and any doubts or guilt he had disappeared.

He took her hand and led her upstairs to his room, which she'd never been in, he realized. He led her over to his bed and urged her to sit down on the bedspread.

She went willingly, staring up at him with trust in her eyes and an expression that he swore was almost shy.

"Are you just going to stare at me, or did you maybe wanna do the whole *get naked* thing?"

"I like the idea of getting naked." He smiled and pulled his shirt off, then popped the fly on his jeans. Slid the zipper down.

He went to sit on the edge of the bed and pulled her tank top over her head. He paused to stroke the curve of her breasts.

"You are so beautiful," he murmured, holding the weight of them in his palms. He leaned forward and licked her nipples. Again, and again. Until the tips were hard and wet. He blew on them lightly, loving the way she trembled and arched her back towards him.

He drew one textured nipple into his mouth again, suckling it while he rolled the other one between his fingers.

Christy sighed and cradled his head to her, her fingers threading through his hair. He loved it when she did that, tugging slightly at his hair and massaging his scalp.

Adam sucked on her nipples harder, loving the soft moans that followed. He lowered her so that she was reclining on the bed, still sucking as he unfastened the buttons on her skirt and slid it down her legs.

Lifting his head, he looked down at her. "I loved those panties you had on earlier."

"I thought you would, cowboy."

"I think the whole bar loved them, too." He laughed, and then laughed harder when her look turned to mortification.

"Oh, thanks for the reminder. I'd forgotten about that." She sighed and wrinkled her nose. "Jeez. Did I really show my ass to everyone in the bar?"

"Your *ruffled, pink ass*, darlin'," he murmured and ran a slow hand down her naked body. His cock hardened further at the soft silkiness of her skin, the way she trembled at his touch.

She covered his hand with her own to still it, and glanced up at him from under her lashes. "Aren't you going to finish getting undressed?"

"Do you want me naked that bad?"

"Yes," she answered bluntly. "I want you naked so I can ride you like I rode that bull."

Adam's amusement faded and his cock lengthened another inch. He stood up and kicked off his jeans and briefs. So much for taking it nice and slow.

"Ah, yes." She reached out to stroke his hard cock. "I've been thinking about this guy all night."

Adam bit back a groan as her hand circled him and then moved firmly up and down his length.

He leaned down to kiss her, keeping it gentle while he sought the warmth of her mouth. Her hand continued to move over him as she rubbed her tongue against his.

Adam groaned and parted her legs, sliding his body between her thighs.

She pushed against his shoulders. "Condom."

Shit. Adam nodded and slid off her again, going to retrieve one from his nightstand. Maybe he could talk her into birth control soon. Lord, how he wanted that hot, wet flesh squeezing his dick without a condom between them.

When he looked back at the bed, she was touching herself and watching him with hooded eyes.

"Hurry back, cowboy." Her smile was lazy. "I want you on top of me, inside me."

"I thought you were riding me?" Adam teased as he rejoined her on the bed, putting on the condom in record time.

"I figured we could alternate." She opened her thighs wider, a blatant invitation for him to come home.

Adam slid between her legs and took a moment to caress the hot slippery folds of her pussy that lay open before him.

"You don't trust that I'm ready?" she teased, the shift in her breathing another indication of her desire for him.

"You're ready. I was just never good at that look but don't touch rule." His fingers became coated with her slick moisture, and he moved them up to rub her swollen clit.

She closed her eyes, moaning in pleasure.

No more. He couldn't wait a second longer. He positioned his cock just outside her entrance, and used his arms to support his body as he slid into her.

She gasped. "Oh, I'll never get used to how completely you fill me." Her hips flexed under his. "You feel so amazing. So right."

Adam couldn't even respond, but the same thought ran through his head. He would never get used to being with her. Even if they'd been together for fifty years.

He pressed deeper. When he was embedded to the hilt, he remained there for a moment just to enjoy the feel of her slippery, tight heat surrounding him.

"Oh, Adam..." She let out a shuddering breath. "Yes."

Their bodies touched from shoulder to toes, the stiff tips of her nipples teasing the hair on his chest.

He withdrew and began to thrust in and out in a steady and slow rhythm, lowering his body enough so he could kiss her again. A slow and sensual kiss that matched the easy pace of their lovemaking.

But soon it wasn't enough. He started rotating his hips to hit deeper and more pleasurable spots for her.

Christy's fingernails clawed down his chest as she bucked under him, lifting her hips to meet each of his deep thrusts.

Then she urged him to roll over while still keeping him inside. She settled in her new position on top.

He watched the drugged look of pleasure on her face and thrust deep inside her again. She leaned back, bringing him to a new angle, and then began circling her hips and doing small rocking movements on him.

His sac tightened at the change in sensation, almost sending him over the edge, but he managed to hold back. Just barely. Instead, he turned his attention to the breasts that were jiggling so enticingly above him.

He reached up and stroked both of her nipples while she rode him and her body clenched around his cock in response.

She picked up her pace and began moving on him in a steady rhythm. Seeing that she was near her pleasure, he reached down between their bodies to make sure she'd go over the edge.

Before he could even touch her though, she climaxed, and the sight of her head thrown back and her simultaneous screams brought him to a quick orgasm.

He came inside her as her body clenched and pulsed around him, milking everything he had. She collapsed on him, laying her cheek over his pounding heart.

So amazing. He closed his eyes and let his hands settle on her hips possessively. *Mine, she's mine.* He kissed her forehead and nuzzled her hair, inhaling the fruity scent of her shampoo.

"I love you," she murmured drowsily.

Warmth spread through his body, and a strange feeling of triumph. Why? This wasn't some stupid game where he got the girl in the end. Even still, his grip on her tightened.

Like a dam with cracks, the doubt slipped through the warmth in his gut. Did she actually mean it? Or was it the alcohol talking? Or maybe the post-sex thing?

He closed his eyes. Biting his tongue before he could say the same words back to her. Hopefully she didn't expect him to.

Apparently she didn't, because he could feel her warm breath on his chest and her steady breathing indicated she was asleep. Or passed out.

Adam pulled her closer and closed his eyes. Tomorrow things could be worked out. He'd talk to Nate about everything, and see if Christy still fancied herself in love in the sobering light of day.

Christy woke up to the sound of birds and the warm feeling of sunshine on the bed. She rolled over, seeking Adam's warmth. Her eyes opened when she didn't find it.

She sat up and looked around the room, but the house was oddly quiet. Her glance fell on the clock beside the bed. It was only six-thirty. Where would he have gone this early?

She lay back against the pillows with a sigh. No matter, he'd return eventually. She snuggled deeper under his incredibly soft sheets and let herself enjoy the moment of being in Adam's bed. His room. His life.

Providing Adam asked her to—and given last night it seemed likely he would—then she probably would stick around. She liked it here. Peppertown. The small town that Nate had felt smothered him was a wide-open paradise to her. She could easily do it. Move here and be happy.

She'd have to give notice to her school, she thought, and then see if there were any openings for a Spanish teacher around town here. Or she could always teach Salsa dancing, but that would require finding a studio to rent and teach at.

She'd need to find an apartment too. Huh. Did they even have apartments here? *I'm going to live outside of the city. Become a certified country girl.* She bit back a laugh, her stomach warming at the thought. Oh, her mom was going to love that.

Love. Christy jerked upright in bed. *Oh. God.* She'd told Adam she loved him last night. Suddenly the silence of the house became more ominous. What if she'd freaked him out by saying those three little words? It wasn't so far-fetched. There were a lot of men who went AWOL when a girl said the L-word.

Christy pushed the sheets off her body and started to climb out of bed.

"Good morning. I brought you breakfast."

Sinking back against the pillows, she dragged the sheet with her as she stared at him. He hadn't left her. And he didn't even look too freaked out.

Her mouth watered at the sight of coffee and muffins on the tray. Not to mention the sexy man holding them.

"How's your head?" Adam asked, walking over to the side of the bed and sitting down.

"My head?" She reached for a muffin and took a bite of the strudel-covered top. "Mmm. Did you make these?"

"Now, you know I can't cook, darlin'."

"Right. So it was either a bakery or your mom."

"Betty's Bakery down on First Street." He set the tray down in front of her and picked up his own mug of coffee. "You had a lot to drink last night. I was thinking you might have a headache."

She caught sight of the bottle of aspirin on the tray and various parts of the evening came back to her.

Oh God! She'd been tossed from the mechanical bull.

Everyone in the bar had seen her ruffled panties. She could feel the heat flooding to her cheeks. Great, now that would be an embarrassing point she'd have to work past if she ended up staying in Peppertown.

"Umm. No, I don't have a headache." She lifted her mug of coffee and took a sip.

"Good. I was worried about you." He dropped a kiss on her forehead. "I'll be back later. I need to run in to work."

"Oh. All right." Disappointment settled in her stomach, but she smiled. "Thank you again for breakfast. And, umm, I'm sorry again about last night."

"Stop worrying about it."

Easier said than done. She shook her head and tore off another piece of muffin, watching his cute behind walk out of the room.

ि

Adam strode inside his house and out of the hot sun. He dragged his wrist across his forehead to wipe off the sheen of sweat. Lord, what a long day. A day where thoughts of Christy had consumed him.

The urge to touch her, hold her in his arms hit strong again.

"Christy?" he called out, heading to the kitchen to pour himself a glass of water.

There was no response and he took a sip of water, frowning. His gaze landed on the kitchen table and he spotted the note there. Strolling over, he picked it up and then smiled.

"So you went to see Mom after all." He set the note back down and drank the rest of the water.

Tempting Adam

Placing the cup in the sink, he sighed and pulled his cell phone out of his pocket. It was time. With Christy out of the house, he didn't have to worry about her overhearing the conversation he was about to have.

He couldn't keep putting it off. He had to know, had to talk to Nate before this thing with Christy went any further. The guilt was at an all-out war with the warm sensation of the possibility that Christy really loved him.

He dialed Nate's number and waited for him to answer.

"Adam?" Nate's voice came through the phone sounding stilted and wary.

"Hey, Nate, how're you doing?"

"How am I?" he repeated and started to laugh, which turned into a groan. "Oh, God, my head hurts. I'm hungover."

Hungover? Was he taking it that hard? Maybe this hadn't been such a mutual thing. Premonition clawed in his gut and his grip tightened on the cell phone.

"Oh, sorry to hear that." He hesitated. "Look. Christy told me you broke up. Do you mind if I ask why?"

"Why?" Nate sounded confused. "Why do you want to know why?"

Because I want to soothe my guilty conscience. "I just...need to."

"I—well, um..." Nate's voice came out a little strange. "I think she said I wasn't good in bed."

Adam frowned. Well, that could certainly be true, with the erectile dysfunction issue Christy had mentioned.

"So that's the entire reason why?"

"Isn't that enough? I mean..." Nate seemed to be thinking about what to say. "She said...she wanted to get married soon, and you know me. I'm just not the marrying kind."

"What?" Adam nearly dropped his phone.

"Uh—you know how some women can get, they always want a ring," Nate went on, talking quicker now and sounding more confident. "We'd been arguing about it for a while. I called to talk to her about it yesterday, but she said it didn't matter and that she'd changed her mind. That it never would have worked out between us anyway."

"I see." The phone Adam held was now at risk of being crushed in his fierce grip.

"I think maybe she met someone else. Which is all right, our relationship wasn't perfect. I just want her to be happy."

"No relationship is perfect," Adam replied automatically, trying to remain calm. "I need to go, call me if you need anything."

"Okay." Nate sounded surprised. "Thanks, Adam. Take care of Christy."

Take care of Christy? Adam hung up the phone. Had Nate suspected their affair? A mixture of emotions hit him at once. Pain, guilt, anger. He shook his head and groaned, clenching his fists.

Everything fell into place. Christy wanted marriage and had realized real fast which brother had the deeper pockets. It could hardly be a coincidence that she'd broken up with Nate the same day she'd realized Adam was a millionaire.

No wonder she'd been in such a snit when she'd told him she was available and he hadn't jumped with joy.

Damn. She'd been playing him the entire time. And he'd fallen right into her hands.

His heart argued the theory, told him Christy wasn't like this—there had to be something he didn't know. *You're a romantic idiot. You see what you want to see.* All he had to do was look at the evidence of the past week.

His stomach twisted and he swallowed against the sudden nausea.

And last night...that hadn't been a heartfelt declaration of love or, hell, even an alcohol-induced one. It had been pure calculation on her part. She says "I love you" and he's supposed to propose.

This wasn't about love. This was about Christy securing a future for herself. And no matter what his feelings were for her, he refused to be a pawn in anyone's game of Life.

What was done could be undone. He ground his teeth together and took a deep breath. No matter how much it would nearly kill him.

He opened his phone again and dialed Christy's cell phone. It rang twice before she answered.

"Hey, you. How's work?"

Her sweet voice rubbed on his raw emotions, he tightened his fingers around the phone.

"Adam? Are you still there?"

"Yeah. I came home early." He cleared his throat. *Do this. You need to do this.* He closed his eyes. "We need to talk."

"Talk?" He could hear the hesitancy in the one word.

"Yeah."

"All right. I'll have your mom bring me back home." She paused. "Then maybe we can do more than just talk, cowboy."

Despite the hurricane of emotions raging through him, his blood stirred at the husky endearment.

"I'll see you soon." He shut the phone, resisting the temptation to call her "darlin'", and let out a ragged breath.

Wiping away any tenderness for her, he gave a stiff nod.

He'd do what he had to do tonight. Nate deserved at least that. If Christy had thought to play them, brother against brother, she deserved nothing less.

Christy stepped inside Adam's house and ran her hands down the blue silk dress she wore. Having lunch with Adam's mom had been enjoyable. A nice way to break up the afternoon. Adam's phone call had set her on edge a bit though.

He'd said he'd wanted to talk. About what? She blinked as the door slammed shut behind her, and let her eyes adjust to the light.

"Hey."

She pressed her hand against her chest and swiveled to the right. Adam sat on the chaise lounge, watching her.

"Hey, yourself." She hesitated and then crossed the room to sit down next to him. "I missed you today."

"Did you now?" He didn't blink, just stared at her with a surprisingly blank expression.

"Bad day at work?" She took his hand and gave it a light squeeze.

He pulled his hand free and she gave a soft gasp, her heart pounded harder.

She ran her tongue across her lips and gave him a closer look, watching as his jaw clenched and unclenched.

"What's going on?" she asked tentatively.

He didn't answer. Instead, he stood up and walked across the room to the foot of the stairs.

She blinked, trying to comprehend what she was seeing as he brought her bags to her and set them at her feet.

The fear hit again, paralyzing her as she lowered her gaze to her bags. Maybe he'd lost it. Completely freaked out in some kind of delayed reaction at her having said "I love you" last night.

"Do you think I'm a complete idiot?"

She jerked her head up. Her mouth went dry and her pulse doubled in time. Had he learned of her and Nate's charade?

She licked her lips. "I'm sorry?"

"You broke up with Nate the same day you found out I was a millionaire." His gaze hardened on her. "Nate can't get it up for you, and I can. Add in the fact that I'm loaded, it all makes sense. You're nothing more than a gold-digging slut."

Christy blinked and her stomach clenched. "*What?*"

"I think you heard me just fine."

"Where is this coming from?" she asked, her voice hoarse. "You know me, Adam. You know I'm not like that."

"I thought I knew you." His jaw clenched. "I really did. But, damn, did you pull the wool over my eyes."

Hell, yeah she had, but not for *that* reason. "All right. Let's have this out, right here, right now."

"It doesn't matter anymore." He gestured to her bags. "I've packed your stuff—"

"You went through my things?" Anger coiled in her belly. This was getting so out of control.

"I'll drop you at your car."

Her eyes narrowed. "Adam—"

"Besides, you really didn't think I'd fall for my brother's hand-me-downs, did you?"

The air locked in her throat and she could feel the blood draining from her face. She kneeled down to pick up her bags, tears blurring her vision.

"I'll drive you to your car." His voice gentled a bit.

"Don't even fucking bother." She adjusted the bags in her hand. "And for your information, your brother can't get it up for *any* woman. He's gay, you asshole."

"Oh, come off it." His brows rose and his mouth tightened. "Don't you think I'd notice if my own brother was gay? That's reaching a bit far."

"Yeah, Adam. I kind of *did* think you'd notice." She gave a sharp laugh and turned away, striding out the door and down the porch.

She let the tears fall now. Damn it, her car wasn't even here. She had to walk back to Adam's parents' house.

Adam... She drew in an unsteady breath. Her heart suddenly felt like it was being pulled from her chest with rusty pliers.

She increased her pace, ignoring the pain of walking in high heels. Too bad she hadn't had a clear enough head to think to put on some decent shoes.

How had she been so wrong about Adam? She'd thought...it didn't matter. Nothing did. Her eyes flooded with tears of self-pity, pain, and anger.

She had gambled for Adam and she had lost. Not just lost, but got the shit kicked out of her.

A car slowed down and finally pulled over in front of her. Christy half-expected it to be Adam, begging for her forgiveness and carrying her back into his truck.

But it was the bartender from last night, an older man with a gentle face.

"Hey there, missy, you need a ride somewhere?" he offered, approaching her.

Christy felt guilt build on top of all her other turbulent emotions. She'd been so rude to him last night and he was offering her a ride?

"If you wouldn't mind," she said through her tears.

"Come on." His voice was kind, his touch gentle as he helped her back to his car. "Where can I drop you?"

"Candace and Steve Young's house." She hesitated. "Do you know where that is?"

"Everybody in town knows the Youngs." He gave her a sympathetic glance, as if he knew who she'd just been with. "I've known Nate and Adam since they were running around in diapers."

"Was Adam as cruel then as he is now?" she asked bitterly.

"Adam? Cruel?" The man shook his head. "I can't say I've ever known him to be cruel."

You're not a woman. Fresh tears welled in her eyes.

"Here we are, missy," the bartender told her and gave her a light pat on her shoulder. "I'm sure it'll work itself out, whatever it is."

"Thank you." She gave a weak smile, deciding not to point out that hell wasn't yet in danger of freezing over.

Christy shut the door to his car and dug into her purse to find her keys. She climbed inside her Beetle and started the engine. It wheezed for a moment before grumbling to life. She looked at the house just as Candace pulled back the curtain to look outside. The curtain fell back into place and Christy had a feeling Adam's mom would be outside soon.

She backed up quickly, wanting to get away and avoid a scene. Sure enough, in her rearview mirror she saw Candace, Steven and... Nate, on the porch. What was Nate doing here? She frowned, but continued out of their driveway.

She pulled onto the main road and didn't look back. She was done with all of them. It was best for everyone if she just cut it clean and left. Apparently they weren't done with her, because her phone started ringing and it was Nate.

Out of a sense of morbid curiosity she decided to answer and see what he could possibly have to say.

"Where are you going?" he demanded.

"Home. Back to Seattle. Back where the whole town doesn't consider me a cheating whore."

"What happened?" Nate asked, sounding wary.

"Does it matter?" She scrubbed a fist over her eyes to ward off more tears. "Adam wants nothing more to do with me."

"He called me a little while ago. I was already on my way over here."

"What?" She gripped the steering wheel tighter and frowned. "When? What did you say?"

"I didn't know what to tell him. We never actually decided what we were going to tell people as to why we broke up."

She wanted to argue, but realized he was right.

"What exactly did you tell Adam?"

"I thought it was a clever answer at the time," he began. "But the more I thought about it, I started to realize it might not have been. I was hoping to straighten things out when I arrived, but I guess I'm too late."

Christy took a deep breath. *Calm. Stay calm.* "What did you tell him? I won't be mad."

"I told him you wanted to get married and I wasn't ready to."

"*What?*"

"Uh, that's not all." He groaned. "Then I told him I tried to talk to you about it and you told me you wanted to break up."

Oh. God. No wonder Adam hated her.

"You're totally pissed, aren't you?"

She couldn't answer yet. If she did, she'd scream yes and smash her cell phone into her dashboard.

"I'm sorry, Christy. Please forgive me," he pleaded. "I didn't think when I said it. I'm hungover and was grouchy from the heat. I guess I caused you to end your fling before you wanted to. But at least you weren't in love with him."

Her silence was met by more silence.

"Oh, Christy," he said carefully. "You were in love with him?"

"Like I said, it doesn't matter," she finally managed to say. "I'm on my way back—damn!"

Her car sputtered, and she managed to get it to the side of the road before it died completely.

"What's wrong?"

"My car just died!" Her vision blurred with more tears. "Could this day get any worse? Come pick me up, Nate! Take me to the nearest bus station."

"I'll be right there. Where are—oh. Adam just walked into the house. I'll call you back."

"Don't you dare hang up on me!" Christy screamed, but she was yelling into dead air.

She swore, climbed out of the Beetle and started walking.

Chapter Eighteen

Adam walked into his parents' house wondering if it were possible to feel like a bigger asshole. He had the beginning of a headache, and his mind kept playing over the genuine hurt and shock in Christy's eyes.

"Adam? Where's Christy?" his mom demanded, speed-walking over to him. "I saw her drive off in her car a minute ago."

"She had to get home to Seattle."

"What did you say to her?" The door slammed and Adam turned to see Nate striding across the room looking one-hundred-percent pissed.

The poor guy must still have feelings for her. His decision to cut her off in an abrupt and harsh manner seemed more justified when he looked at the raw emotion on his brother's face.

"Don't worry about it, Nate." He went to sit down on the couch. "She's gone."

"Yeah, I got that part." Nate glared and came to stand in front of him. "I want to know what you said to her."

Adam glanced up at him, not bothering to hide the pain and fury in his own gaze.

"You want to know? Fine," he said harshly. "I told her she was a gold-digging slut, and I didn't want my brother's hand-me-downs."

His mother gasped from across the room. "Adam William Young. You didn't!"

Their dad stepped in from the kitchen, a grim look on his face. "Adam? I raised you better than that. You didn't really, did you?"

Christ. Adam shook his head. He was a grown man in his thirties. He should not have to answer to his family.

"Why would you say that?" Nate demanded. "Why would you say something so freaking mean?"

"Because she was using us," Adam snapped. "Can't you all see it? Christy was in a *blissful* relationship with Nate for over a year. Then she met me and realized I was the one with the money, and she couldn't jump into bed with me fast enough."

"Blissful relationship? Adam," his mom choked again, "are you completely blind?"

"So you and Christy *were* sleeping together?" His dad's mouth curved into a grin.

Adam blinked. His dad was happy about that? What the hell was going on here?

"Oh, for Christ's sake," Nate snapped. "I'm gay. All right? I'm gay."

Adam swallowed against the bile that worked its way up his throat. He struggled to breathe, feeling as if he'd been slugged in the gut.

His mom sighed. "Well, tell us something we don't know, son."

Adam and Nate both turned sharply to look at their parents.

"You...knew?" Nate's voice rang with disbelief.

Christy had been serious earlier? Adam shook his head. "But you and Christy were dating—"

"Christy was never my girlfriend," Nate muttered. "I asked her to pretend to be when you guys came out to visit."

Their mom laughed, smiling. "I told you, Steven. Now hand over my ten dollars."

"What?" Nate blinked, his gaze jerking from their mom to their dad.

"I knew she wasn't really your girlfriend all along, Nate. And I bet your dad ten dollars you were just trying to convince us—or, heck, yourself—that you preferred girls." Their mom walked over to Nate and drew him into her arms. "Sweetheart, we've suspected you were gay since you were a teenager. And I want you to know we're completely all right with it."

Adam blinked, and shook his head. His *parents* had known?

His dad glanced over at Adam. "And once we realized which brother was *really* in love with Christy, we figured we'd give Adam that last little nudge. Termite problem? Bah, we've never had any problems with termites."

In love with Christy. He closed his eyes and groaned. Lord, he was an idiot. He *was* in love with her...and he'd just sent her packing in the most brutal way.

"Let me get this straight." Adam turned to his brother and grabbed his shoulders. "You and Christy were never together?"

"That's right."

"So this entire time you've been gay, and she's been a single woman?" Nausea swept through him and the guilt tripled.

"That's right."

"Well, hell," he muttered.

"Where are you going?" Nate demanded when Adam strode towards the door.

"To make things right, and to apologize until I'm blue in the face."

"Her car broke down about two minutes after she left here," Nate yelled after him as he walked out the door.

Adam noted the information as he hopped into his truck and roared out of the driveway. He drove down the highway that led out of town—and also back to his house—and saw her Beetle a few minutes later.

He pulled up behind it and parked, jumping down from the truck to find her. Her car was empty. He glanced down the road and saw a silhouette under one of the street lamps.

"Christy!" He smiled grimly when the figure turned around to look at him. The smile disappeared when she turned and started running in the opposite direction.

"Hold up, darlin'!" He took off at a run after her.

But she didn't hold up, if anything she increased her pace. How the hell a woman in heels could outrun him was beyond his understanding, but she did. In fact she reached his property, ran past his house and straight for the lake.

"Where are you going?" He was still about a hundred yards behind her. "Hold up, we need to talk."

She didn't even look back, just ran straight out onto the dock on the lake. He saw her bending down and fidgeting with something, and then she jumped off the dock and into the rowboat below.

Damn. He increased his pace, reaching her just as she shoved herself away from the dock and began floating towards the middle of the lake.

"Ah, darlin'." He shook his head at her. "That was a downright foolish thing to do."

"Why? It keeps me away from you, you arrogant piece of—"

"Because, you don't have any oars..."

Christy glanced down in the boat she was in, and bit back a groan. God, there really weren't any oars in here. Only she would set herself adrift in a boat without oars. If that weren't enough, the wind was picking up and she was getting blown farther away from the dock.

"So toss them to me!" she screamed in frustration.

"I got muscle," he drawled. "But not enough to toss an oar halfway across a lake."

"Fine. I don't need them." She folded her arms across her chest. "Just leave me alone. I'll eventually reach the other side. When I do I'll get out and walk to the bus station."

"I can't do that."

Christy gave a chortle of disbelief when he dove into the lake fully clothed and started swimming towards her.

"What the hell are you doing?" She stood up.

"I told you," he yelled when his face appeared out of the water while doing the crawl stroke. "We need to talk."

Christy sat back down on the wooden bench seat of the boat and sighed. She rolled her eyes and glanced over the water and the land beyond it. His property once again took her breath away.

What was she doing? She shook her head. Admiring his home while the man she hated—or loved—swam fully clothed across a lake to reach her?

Two hands clasped the side of the boat and sent it rocking wildly.

Christy leaned forward to grasp his hands, and help pull him into the small wooden boat.

"Why are you back?" She gave him a hard glance. "Surely you're still convinced I'm just a gold-digging slut."

"Ah, darlin', I'm so sorry," he muttered. "I wasn't thinking right. I said some real nasty things just so you'd run away and hate me."

"Hey, good job. It worked."

"I just have one question for you." He pulled her resisting body onto his lap. "What the hell made you agree to pretend to be Nate's girlfriend?"

Christy stopped squirming away from his wet body and stared at him, her jaw dropping in surprise.

"You know?"

"I know." He stroked a hand down the side of her cheek.

"How?"

"Nate told us tonight," he admitted. "He let me have it, too. For treating you like..."

"Yeah, what am I doing?" She tried to break free again. "You basically called me sloppy seconds and here I am thinking of taking you back? I don't think so, buddy. That was just downright cruel, Adam. That side of you was—"

"Ugly? God awful?" He tightened his hold on her. "I know, Christy. And I'm so sorry. I don't know what came over me, except I was jealous, hurting bad, and just completely worked up."

She stopped squirming and took a ragged breath. "Adam..."

"I trust you, Christy, and that's the kicker of it all. I should have believed you when you told me. I'm an idiot."

Her anger melted a little and she relaxed in his arms, lowering her lashes. "Well, at least you admit it."

"But why? Why would you ever agree to go through with such a pointless charade with Nate?"

She shook her head in disgust. "Because I'm a sucker who has a hard time saying no."

"No, you're a faithful friend who Nate took advantage of. He's very lucky to have you, and I think he realized that tonight when he tried to make things right."

"Did he succeed?" She met his gaze.

"Come on, Christy. You know how much you mean to me."

"How do I know that?" she asked in disbelief, even as hope sparked inside her. "You've never told me."

"I didn't want to admit it, I suppose." He nuzzled the side of her neck and she bit back a groan.

"Hold on, Adam. I need to know." She pushed back as far in his arms as he'd let her go. "How did everyone take the news about Nate?"

His mouth curled into a lazy smile. "Well, apparently the folks already knew and were just waiting for him to jump out of the closet. And more than that..." He ran the pad of his thumb over her lips. "They suspected our feelings for each other."

"They did? Were they mad?" Her heart skipped at his touch.

"Not at all. They approved wholeheartedly—even made up the termites excuse so you'd have to stay with me."

"No kidding? See, I knew I liked your parents." She lifted her gaze to his. "How did you react to Nate's announcement? Once you got past the realization that I was right."

Adam's slow smile sent her heart thumping. "It was the best news I've ever heard."

Her eyes widened. "Why?"

"Because now I don't have to feel guilty about being in love with you."

Christy's eyes filled with tears again, but for all the right reasons this time.

"You mean that?"

"'Course I do, darlin'," he murmured and gave her a slow and thorough kiss.

When he lifted his head from hers, he didn't need to hold her anymore. She was holding him, wrapping her arms around his neck with a sigh.

"Would you protest too much if I moved to Seattle?" he asked.

"I don't want you to move to Seattle."

"Oh." He frowned. "You just want me to visit every now and then?"

"No."

Adam drew back slightly, and she saw the real look of uncertainty in his eyes.

"Are you telling me that you don't want me any more?" His voice was quiet.

Christy smiled. "Come on, cowboy. You swam across a lake fully clothed to reach me. How could I possibly say no to you?"

The tension in his body eased with his soft laughter. "Then what are you saying, Christy?"

"I want to move over here," she murmured, tracing his lips with her finger. "I'll get my own place—"

"I'd rather you live with me."

"Okay, I'll live with you."

"But what about your job?" He frowned again. "I'd hate to ask you to leave."

"Trust me, it's a lot easier to relocate a teacher than an

orchard. And besides, I kind of like it here."

"You do?" he asked, slipping a hand under her dress to stroke over her thigh.

"Mm-hmm." She pressed a kiss to the side of his neck and undid the first button on his denim shirt. "You know, you might want to get out of those soaking clothes. We wouldn't want you to catch a cold."

"That sounds like a pretty smart idea." He helped her nimble fingers along. "You ever made love in a rowboat, darlin'?"

"No," she whispered, placing a light kiss on his mouth. "But there's always a first time."

"I'll try to make sure you don't get any splinters," Adam told her, unzipping her dress.

"That's what I love about you, cowboy. You're a true gentleman," Christy murmured and pulled his mouth back down to hers to seal the deal.

About the Author

To learn more about Shelli Stevens, please visit www.shellistevens.com. Send an email to Shelli at shelli@shellistevens.com or join her Yahoo! group to join in the fun with other readers as well as Shelli Stevens!

http://groups.yahoo.com/group/shellistevens

GREAT CHEAP FUN

Discover eBooks!

THE FASTEST WAY TO GET THE HOTTEST NAMES

Get your favorite authors on your favorite reader, long before they're out in print! Ebooks from Samhain go wherever you go, and work with whatever you carry—Palm, PDF, Mobi, and more.

Samhain Publishing Ltd

WWW.SAMHAINPUBLISHING.COM